the way we fall

CASSIA LEO

The Way We Fall

First Edition
Copyright © 2015 by Cassia Leo

All rights reserved.

Editing by Red Adept Edits.

Copyediting by Marianne Tatom.

Cover art by Sarah Hansen, Okay Creations.

Interior design by Angela McLaurin, Fictional Formats.

ISBN 13: 978-1507704530
ISBN 10: 1507704534

the way we fall

For my faithful beta readers.

Prologue

Lies are comforting. Soft blankets we wrap around our hearts. We roll around in them like fat, happy pigs. Gorging on their decadence. We prefer lies, though we claim otherwise. Trust me. If ignorance is bliss, believing lies is orgasmic.

I should know. I'd subsisted on a steady diet of lies and orgasms while Houston and I were together. And now that he was standing before me, five and a half years after the breakup, six-foot-four inches of solid muscle and caramel-brown hair, offering me my first dose of reality, part of me wondered whether my body would reject it.

Houston sighs as he looks me in the eye. "Rory, I came here because I told you I would tell you the truth and I intend to keep my word."

"The truth about *what?*" I spit back, imbuing my words with caustic venom, hoping he'll feel just a fraction of the agony he's inflicted on me. "It's over Houston. There is no truth that needs to be spoken anymore."

He shakes his head, his blue eyes filled with regret. "I wish that were true."

He reaches into his back pocket and my stomach drops out. My limbs becomes heavy as I watch him retrieve a white envelope. I think part of me knows what's inside that envelope. Has always known. But lies are powerful. And it seems Houston's lies had the power to make me stop looking for answers when they were right in front of me, tucked away in the warmth of his back pocket.

"She left a note."

My eyes are locked on the envelope as memories swirl in my vision. The first night Houston and I slept together. The hours that came before. I begin ticking off the lies one by one, but when I move past our first night together, the lies mount up too quickly. A mountain of fiction too high for me to see over.

"Not Tessa. Hallie," he says, mistaking my horror for confusion.

The anger sets my blood on fire. I land a hard shove in the center of his chest. "I hate you!"

"I didn't want you to read it until you were strong enough."

Skippy barks as I pound on Houston's chest, half-expecting to hear a hollow thump where his heart should be. He drops the letter and grabs my wrists to stop the onslaught of violence.

"That's not for you to decide!" I shout, my voice strangled by the force of this truth. "How could you keep that from me?"

"I was just trying to protect you."

A primal roar issues from deep in my throat. "I wish you would stop protecting me! If it weren't for your stupid protection, I wouldn't be picking up the pieces of my life again."

His jaw tenses at my accusation, the muscle twitching furiously. "I need you to read it while I'm here. I… I won't leave until you've read the whole thing. Then you'll understand why."

Yanking my wrists out of his grasp, I shoo Skippy away so I can grab the letter off the floor. But he follows me as I sink down onto the sofa, hopping onto the cushion next to me, his sixty-pound black Labrador body pressed against my side. As if he can sense that I'm going to need him there.

Houston sits on the edge of the coffee table facing me, our knees inches apart, his gaze locked on the letter in my hands. I try to read his expression, try to see beyond the hardened grief and obvious regret for any indication as to what I'm about to read. What did

Hallie confess in this letter that would make him think he had to lie to me for more than five years? But I see nothing.

He looks up from the envelope and our eyes meet. My heart thumps loudly, a riotous drum heightening the sense of foreboding that grips me. The anticipation crackles in the air and Houston's blue eyes narrow as he hardens himself against the intensity of the moment.

I let my gaze fall to the name scrawled on the outside of the envelope: Houston. The shaking begins suddenly, my hands trembling as if the letter I'm holding is as heavy as the Earth. But it's not heavy, it's just real. It's his name in her handwriting. In her final moments, she turned to him, not me.

I clutch the letter to my chest as tears burn hot streaks down my face, my throat a hard painful mass of anguish. Carefully, I slide the folded letter out of the envelope. The moment I see the words *Dear Houston*, the room seems to tilt on its side, throwing me off balance. But I swallow my nausea and keep reading, ripping my way through five pages, front and back, the sentences feeding into my heart like a never-ending news ticker, getting bleaker and more vile with each passing moment. Until I finally reach Hallie's parting words and magma explodes in my belly, searing my throat.

I leap off the sofa, racing for the bathroom, slamming the door behind me. The meager half-cup of oatmeal I ate this morning launches from my mouth as I grip the porcelain. More retching as milky liquid spews forth, my arms shaking as sweat sprouts over my neck, sending a chill through me.

A knock at the door, followed by more retching until I'm empty of everything. All the warm, comforting lies replaced by a single cold, empty truth.

Another knock at the door.

"Go away!" I wail, my voice a shrieking rasp.

The click of the knob turning. The tick of Skippy's nails against the tile floor as he comes to me. My diaphragm compresses angrily in my chest, attempting to rid my body of the truth. A few deep breaths and the dry heaving finally stops. I fall back, my shoulder blades pressed against the hard bathtub as I try to catch my breath.

Skippy is gone, but Houston is still there, as solid and real as the aching truth gnawing at my insides. He looks down at me, his eyes filled with regret so fiercely tangible, I could probably use it to carve out my heart. If I hadn't already given it to him thirteen years ago.

This is not the way the story of us is supposed to go.

Part 1: Denial

"Even when we want to forget,
our scars have a way of
reminding us where we've been."

Rory

MY NAME IS Aurora Charles, but everyone calls me Rory. Rory Charles. It's the kind of name that conjures up scuffed knees and messy ponytails pulled through the back of a dirty baseball cap, but I could not have been further from a tomboy. In fact, when I was a child, the neighbors would sometimes come check on me because they hadn't seen me playing outside in days. With a book or pencil and paper in hand, I could spend weeks indoors by myself, crafting stories or getting lost in my favorite authors' fictional worlds. I always preferred the comfort of armchair adventures over the outdoor variety. Then, five years ago, everything changed.

I've spent most of those years trying to make sense

of the most beautiful and miserable time of my life. But now I have Skippy to help me put it all behind me. Skippy's always there waiting for me when I get home, ready with a sloppy kiss and all. And he never disappoints me or rejects me. He's my new best friend and soul mate.

I open the door of the dog crate and Skippy prances inside, quickly settling himself down on the plush green dog pillow. His furry black tail wags behind him, splashing in the bowl of water sitting on the floor at the back of the crate. I slip my hand into the wire enclosure and he gently licks the liver treat off my palm.

"Good boy, Skip," I coo, scratching him behind the ears as he looks up at me with those wide chocolate-brown eyes that almost seem hazel against his black fur.

Skippy is my two-year-old black Labrador retriever, adopted from a local shelter when he was five months old and still small enough to fit in my backpack. Nowadays, Skip is a hefty sixty-eight pounds and he prefers riding in my car to riding on my back. When I'm not working, Skip and I do everything together. We frequent all the dog-friendly cafés in Goose Hollow and downtown Portland. We go to the dog park where he plays with his best friend, a four-year-old boxer named Greenland, and his girlfriend Nema, a two-year-old Portuguese water dog.

"I'll be back in a few hours. Love you."

His tongue laps at my palm in what I deem a show

of affection or appreciation, but in reality he's probably just trying to get the crumbs left behind by the liver treat. It's easy to anthropomorphize our pets. We love them. We tend to assign human characteristics to almost anything we love. We name our pets, our cars, even our body parts, as if they have a life of their own. So what does it mean when we have trouble naming something? That we don't love it? How about when you're trying to name a piece of art?

This is one of the few topics that was never covered in college when I studied creative writing. How do you come up with a title for a book, a poem, a play? Is it the same way you name a baby or a pet? Do you pick your favorite title and stick with it? Or do you assign it a title that has a special meaning?

My mother likes to brag that she named me Aurora because I was conceived in Alaska under the northern lights. It's a good story, whether or not it's true. But it doesn't help me one bit. I began writing my book five years ago on an uneventful day, under a cloudless summer sky while riding the train home from the University of Oregon.

Maybe I should name my book *Uneventful Day*. Yes, I'm sure readers would clamor to bookstores for that one.

Of course, that day was only uneventful because my life had blown up a week before and there was nothing good left to salvage from the wreckage. I had no choice but to head home for the summer with my head slung low and my tail between my legs.

I grab my bike helmet off the dining table, ignoring the car keys sitting in the glazed blue dish on the kitchen counter. A hacking sound gets my attention and I sigh when I see Skippy has vomited his morning meal onto the green doggy bed. I let him out of the crate and work as fast as I can to scrub most of the vomit off in the kitchen sink. Then I grab the old dog bed I keep in my closet as a spare and lay it down inside the crate.

After I call my mom and ask her to come check on Skippy while I'm gone, I head out the front door of my one-bedroom apartment in Goose Hollow, a small community in Southwest Portland with a spirited car-free culture. I get in the elevator and press the button for the lower terrace level. When the stainless steel doors slide open, I slip the helmet over my head and buckle it tightly under my chin, wincing as I pull one of my auburn hairs out of the clasp. It's a beautiful August day in Portland, Oregon. Perfect day to ride to work.

I reach the bike storage room near the gym and laundry facilities, and enter my code on the digital padlock securing my bike to the wall rack. Pulling the bike off the wall, I double-check that the straps on my backpack are nice and tight. Then I hop on and set off toward the bridge. The vomiting incident has made me ten minutes late. I need to ride my ass off today.

I hit some gridlock on the way, so I arrive at

Zucker's grocery store on Belmont twenty-three minutes late for my five-hour shift. After hastily locking up my bike in the employee rack behind the store, I enter through the back door. The refrigerated air blasts me in the face and my heated skin bristles at the change in temperature. The warehouse is always freezing and smells of stale lettuce. Edwin, the warehouse supervisor, waves at me from behind the window looking into his office where he's speaking to Minnie, the inventory-slash-payroll clerk.

I wave back and power walk to the time clock to punch in before Edwin can come outside to make small talk and realize I'm late. I tuck my green T-shirt bearing the grocery store logo—a beige Z in the middle of a circle—into my black skinny jeans and head straight for Jamie's office.

Jamie Zucker is the great-granddaughter of Winifred Zucker, the woman who opened the first Zucker's market in 1948 at the ripe age of forty-three. Their family suffered greatly through the Depression. Then Winifred lost her husband, Jacob Zucker, in World War II, leaving her to care for the twins, Jeffrey and John, by herself. Winifred, known to most as "Winnie," worked day and night for four years as a seamstress to save enough money to open her own shop. When the twins were old enough, they took over the market and turned it into a small chain of natural foods stores. Winnie insisted they would never sell the mass-produced junk she saw on the shelves of the big-box supermarkets. They struggled through the '80s and '90s when America experienced a cheap junk food explosion, but the organic food movement of the 21st century breathed new life into their business. And they were now opening their fifth location in East Portland, which Jamie would be running mostly by herself.

Jamie was only twenty-six, but she'd been working at Zucker's for ten years. Her grandfather, John Zucker, still came in once in a while to see how Jamie was doing. He was really there to check how she was running the store. Though it appeared on the outside that he had little faith in her, you could see by the way his eyes lit up in her presence that there was no one he adored more than Jamie. I sometimes wondered what it would feel like to have a grandfather, or even a father, who looked at me like that.

I stride purposefully past the displays of organic Braeburn apples on my left and the dairy case on my right into the rear-right corner of the store. Reaching the office, I knock three times and hear an *Oh, my God!* before Jamie yanks the door open.

"Oh, my God! I can't believe I didn't think of this," she says, her freckled cheeks flushed red and her blue eyes wide with horror. "I need you to pretend to be me."

"What?" I chuckle as she pulls me behind her desk toward the black leather office chair.

"Sit," she commands. "Just hear me out."

She takes a seat in one of the visitor chairs on the other side of the desk, where I normally sit. She pushes her hand through her thin blonde hair as she stares at me, biting her lip as she contemplates what she's going to say. I can't help staring at her one crooked tooth, the top-left pointy cuspid that hangs slightly over her bottom lip.

"Jamie, what's going on? You're sort of freaking me out."

"Rory, I need you to do something for me. As a friend."

A friend? Jamie and I are not enemies, but we're far from friends. We're only two years apart in age, but we're from two different worlds. I graduated from the University of Oregon with a degree in English—with a minor in creative writing—and she dropped out of high school to manage a grocery store. She's engaged to her high school sweetheart. I'm not dating anyone and I never had a high school sweetheart, unless you count the hopeless unrequited crush I had on my best friend's older brother.

Still, even if Jamie's tossing the word *friend* around to get me to do something for her, it does feel good to be needed.

"What do you need?"

She sighs with relief. "I have a meeting with a supplier today. He's coming in to pitch, but Grandpa John's coming. I don't want him to see the guy."

"Why? Isn't he the one who said you needed to keep the selections fresh, or something like that?"

"It's the guy from the beer company coming to discuss the joint venture for the wine bar. Grandpa is dead set against it, but the board is pushing for it."

My heart thumps painfully as I realize what she's asking me.

Management at Zucker's markets has spent the past two years discussing a project to turn some of their in-store espresso cafés into bars that sell wine, beer, and coffee. They'll do wine and beer tastings on Friday and Saturday nights. The bars are being opened only in the locations with a high walk score. A walk score is a rating given to a city based on how easy it is to get around without a car. Goose Hollow has a walk score of 90, which is higher even than New York City. All the board members agreed that the uptown shopping center in Goose Hollow is the perfect area to implement the wine bar idea. Then someone suggested they implement it across all their Portland stores and suddenly our store has been seeing a flurry of meetings over the past few weeks. Apparently, Grandpa John is not supposed to know about these meetings.

I want to get up from Jamie's chair and leave. I didn't realize how safe I felt in my cashier position until now.

"Jamie, I can't pretend to be you. I don't know anything about this wine bar deal."

She holds out her hands to stop me when I attempt to stand. "You don't have to know anything. And you don't really have to pretend to be me. Just thank him for coming and ask him to take a seat. Then you can just sit there and nod and look pretty while he pitches you his beer. I'll try to get Grandpa out of here as quickly as possible. As soon as he's gone, I'll come in and take over."

My entire body tenses with nervous energy just imagining this scenario, but I can't leave her hanging. She's my boss. And it *does* seem like a fairly simple favor to grant.

I draw in a deep breath and let it out slowly. "Sure. I think I can handle that."

"Thank you!" she shrieks as she leaps out of the chair. "You stay here. I'll go out front and wait until the guy gets here, and hope he doesn't get here at the same time as Grandpa."

I lean forward in the leather swivel chair as I watch her leave. She closes the door behind her and my heart races at the thought of what will happen the next time that door opens. Will it be Jamie? Will it be the beer guy? Will it be Grandpa? How will I explain sitting on this side of the desk if it is Grandpa John?

Too many questions for too small of a task. This is nothing. It will be over in a few minutes and I'll be able to get to work.

Leaning back in the chair, I close my eyes and take

another deep breath. The knock at the door startles me. I almost trip and fall in my haste to get out of the chair and answer the door. I manage to catch myself by grabbing on to the edge of the desk, but the damage is done. My nerves are ratcheting up again.

I shake out my arms like a prizefighter getting ready to enter the ring. Reaching for the door handle, I force my lips into a smile, then I open the office door.

I'm frozen at the sight of him.

Rory

HOUSTON CAVANAUGH.

The first boy I ever loved. And *boy*, did I love him a long time. I loved him until he was a man. I loved him until he loved me back. At least, I *thought* he loved me.

His eyes narrow and he appears confused for a moment. "Jamie?"

My heart drops to my feet.

He doesn't even remember me.

"No," I say with far too much emotion.

"Oh, my God. I'm sorry. I… I know you."

I clutch my chest, unable to breathe. Then his eyes widen with what can only be described as pure terror.

"Rory? Aurora?"

I let out a sharp puff of air. "Yeah."

His lips are still moving. I want to hear what he's saying, but my thoughts are pounding in time with my heart. Images flash in my mind: our bodies tangled in his sheets; the breakfast bar littered with sticky shot glasses and empty beer bottles; my empty dorm.

"Rory?"

I blink a few times to focus on his face and he looks at the floor, as if the weight of our history is pulling his head down.

"I'm sorry. Maybe I should come back later."

"What? No!"

He looks up, startled by my outburst.

"I mean, you came to talk about the contract, so... let's talk. I'm..." I nod toward the chair for him to sit down, then I close the office door behind him. "I'm sorry for spacing out. I was just a little surprised to see you." I take a seat in Jamie's chair and yelp as it begins to tip backward. "Shit!"

Houston laughs as I scoot forward and lean my elbows on the desk, hoping he doesn't notice how the sound of his laughter makes the hairs on my arms stand up.

"Sorry. Obviously, I don't sit on this side of the desk very often, but Jamie didn't want to reschedule this appointment. She should be here shortly."

"You don't need to apologize." The left corner of his mouth pulls up in his signature half smile and I grit my teeth against the surge of emotions welling up inside me. "I'm actually kind of glad we ran into each other."

"Really? You hardly remembered me a minute ago."

He chuckles again. "Yeah, sorry about that. I was just surprised."

I can't argue with this when I just used the same excuse. But it's no more true coming from his lips than it is from mine. We're not *surprised* to see each other. We're *terrified.*

All the times I've imagined running into Houston, I never once imagined he wouldn't recognize me. I haven't changed much. I still have the same long auburn hair he used to bury his face in and twist around his fingers. I'm still carrying the extra ten pounds I put on my freshman year at UO, my *softness*, he used to call it. I still don't wear a lot of makeup, though back then I avoided makeup because I never knew when I was going to burst into tears. Now I avoid it because I'm comfortable in my skin. This is who I am. If someone doesn't like me—or recognize me—that's *their* problem.

I swallow the lump in my throat and force a smile. "So, Houston—would you rather I call you Hugh?"

He flashes me an uncomfortable smile, but it takes him a moment to respond. "Houston is fine."

His family always called him Hugh, but he hated it. I always made it a point to call him Houston. Every time I said his name it was like a promise to be true to him. The real Houston. I wish I had known then that you can't promise to be true to a ghost. Ghosts aren't real.

"So... you're the beer guy?" I say, trying to break the awkward silence.

"The beer guy? Is that how I'm referred to around here?"

Houston's gaze is focused on the desk so he doesn't have to look me in the eye. His elbows rest on the arms of the chair and his hands are clasped in front of him. That's when I notice the wedding ring.

"You're married," I blurt out before I can stop myself.

He looks up, his eyes locking on mine, then nods just enough for me to notice.

My eyes and sinuses sting and I blink a few times. "What's her name? I mean, that's... that's great."

Shit. What is wrong with me?

He stares at the desk again, unsure how to respond to this. "Yeah, I guess. Um... Are *you* married?"

For some reason, I glance down at my hands where they rest on top of a stack of invoices on Jamie's desk, as if I'll suddenly find a wedding ring on my finger, too.

"No, I'm not married." I draw in another breath and let it out slowly as I try to think of a new topic. "You're still making beer?"

In college, Houston made his own line of homemade ale, which he called Barley Legal, since barely anyone who drank it was over twenty-one. It was very popular with the frats. I still remember the way our apartment would smell like yeast and alcohol after his weekend "tasting" parties. I'm surprised I still remember the name of the beer and the smell, considering I was pretty wasted through the last six months of my freshman year, the months we were together.

"Yep. And it's still Barley Legal."

"You kept the name?"

"Couldn't let it go."

My breath hitches at these words. They're so similar to the last words he whispered in my ear five years ago as I lay in bed pretending to sleep. *I love you, but we need to let it go.*

He doesn't seem to catch the similarity. Maybe he doesn't even remember the last words he spoke to me. How can he be so different when he looks exactly the same? The shock of caramel-brown hair on his head still has the natural ribbons of sandy blond running through it. His blue eyes still sparkle when he talks about his homemade creations, though they're probably not homemade anymore. He still looks like the guy who took my mind and body to places they'd never been. But there's something very different about him. He seems subdued. Defeated.

"Rory," he says, just loud enough to break through my thoughts. "How have you been?"

I don't know why he's asking this question ten minutes into our conversation, so I shrug. "Fine. I graduated two years ago. I changed my major after...

Anyway, I got my degree in English—minor in creative writing. I've been working on a book in my spare time."

His face lights up at this news. "A book? That's *awesome*. You were always a great writer."

"Well, probably not *great*, but I graduated."

He smiles at my modesty. "You were great. I'm sure you're even better now."

My smile fades. Is it okay to accept praise from him now that he's married? Is it okay to *want* his praise when I've lived without it for five years?

My phone vibrates in my pocket and I pull it out to see who it is. My mom's cell number flashes on the screen. I usually send her calls to voicemail while I'm at work and check them on my lunch break, but I *did* ask her to check on Skippy today.

I contemplate answering her call, if only to escape the awkwardness of my conversation with Houston, but I hit the reject button. If it's an emergency, she'll send me a text. I've told her multiple times to text me in the case of an emergency, since I'm almost always with a customer when she gets the urge to call.

I look up and Houston's jaw is clenched as he stares at the food-handling certificates hanging on the wall of the office.

"It was my mom," I say, not sure why I feel the need to mention this. "Probably just wants to tell me I'm out of coffee or something."

"You still live with your mom and dad?"

"No. *God*, no. My parents divorced two weeks after… we broke up. My mom and I moved to Portland two years ago. She has her own apartment now, but she checks on my dog while I'm at work."

He smiles at my reaction and my stomach flutters. Then, I find myself wondering what shifted between us in the last minute or two, because I'm beginning to wish we could sit here talking like this forever. But any minute now Jamie is going to walk through that office door and relieve me of this meeting.

"How long have you worked here?" Houston asks as he leans back in his chair, getting a bit more comfortable.

He's dressed in jeans and a brown T-shirt bearing the logo of his company. The shirt clings to his biceps and pectoral muscles. I try not to think of the nights I fell asleep with his arms around me and my cheek pressed against his solid chest. The fact that he wore a T-shirt and jeans to a pitch meeting proves he hasn't changed. He's still the laid-back guy everyone wants to share a beer with. And if he hasn't changed, I should stop letting my mind wander to our past.

"I've worked here a little more than a year," I reply. "I interned at the *Oregonian* for a while after graduation, but I got tired of living with my mom and never having money. I applied for this job on a whim, but it ended up working out. I'm union, so I make enough to live in a one-bedroom nearby and still feed myself and Skippy."

"Skippy?"

"My dog."

"Oh."

The desk phone rings and I contemplate not answering it, but it could be Jamie calling me from somewhere else in the store. "Jamie Zucker's office. How may I help you?"

"Rory! Skip passed out and I can't wake him up." My mom is frantic and I can tell by the thickness in her throat that she's crying. My mom never cries, and the mere sound of it makes my heart race.

"What? What's going on? What happened?" I stand suddenly and Houston's smile disappears as he stands, too.

"I don't know. The apartment was pretty warm when I came inside. I don't think your air conditioner's working. He was just lying there in the crate, so I put some ice in his water bowl and put it next to his face so he could drink. He drank the whole bowl, then he passed out! Oh, my God. Did I do something wrong? I was just trying to cool him down. I swear, I didn't mean to do anything. I'm sorry, Rory. I'm so sorry."

"Oh, no. How long has he been out?"

"About twelve minutes now."

"Is he breathing?"

"I don't know. I think so."

"I'll be right there."

I hang up the desk phone and grab my cell off the stack of invoices. Then I scroll through my contacts searching for the number to Skip's vet as Houston follows me out of the office.

"*Shit!* I rode my bike today. It will take me at least twenty-five minutes to get there."

"I can take you," Houston immediately volunteers.

I gaze into his eyes, knowing that every second I hesitate could mean the difference between life and death for my best friend.

Suddenly, the memories come flooding back to me from the day my world was turned upside down five and a half years ago. The day I found Houston standing outside my dorm refusing to let me inside. The day Houston became my protector and my downfall.

My finger hovers over the call button, then I grab Houston's arm as he begins walking straight toward Grandpa John and Jamie, who are both standing at register three talking to Kenny, another cashier.

Houston glances down at his arm where my fingers are curled around his firm bicep. I quickly let it go.

"Sorry, but we can't go that way. We have to go through the back. Hurry."

He follows me into the warehouse and out through the back door.

"What about your meeting?" I mention as we skitter like mice along the back wall of the store.

"I'll work it out," he replies quickly.

We turn right at the back corner of the building into a small service alley that reeks of trash and stale beer.

"Where are you parked?" I ask.

"Right out front. Don't you need to tell your boss you're leaving?"

"I'll call her after I call the vet."

We make it to the end of the alley and Houston grabs my arm before I can walk out onto the sidewalk. "Rory, wait."

I glance down at his fingers, which are curled around my forearm the same way mine were curled around his bicep a minute ago, and I instantly grow impatient. "What?"

He's silent for a moment, then he lets go of me. "Nothing. Let's go."

I follow closely behind him as we approach his shiny, pearl-white SUV. The sight of it makes my stomach curdle. Not because it's a gas-guzzler, but because his wife probably sat next to him inside this car, holding his hand, stroking his skin. Maybe they've even had sex in there.

I know I shouldn't care. I haven't seen or heard from Houston in five years and here he is going out of his way to help me—again. As if the past five years never happened.

He opens the passenger door for me and I grit my teeth as I climb inside, holding my breath to block out the heady scent of beige leather.

Shutting the door after me, he rounds the front of the car and smoothly climbs into the driver's seat.

"Where are we going?" he asks, unable to hide the hint of enthusiasm in his voice.

I stare straight ahead and think, *I wish I knew.*

Houston

I STARE AT the dashboard so I can't see her face. She looks the same as she did five years ago, and back then that face had the power to knock the breath out of me. The curve of her cheekbones, the fullness of her lips, the softness of her skin. She was the drug that numbed the pain, but only temporarily. I just have to keep reminding myself of that so I don't do anything stupid, like telling her the truth.

We may only ever have one great, passionate love. If I had one, it would definitely be Rory. But sometimes it's best to leave that kind of love in the past. Still, there's so much unfinished business between us. As I watch her from the corner of my eye, I wonder if this chance encounter is the opportunity for absolution I've been hoping for the past five years.

"Hold on," she says as she presses the cell phone to her ear. "Hello? Yes, is Dr. Heinlein in the office today?... My dog is unconscious and I need to bring him in. It's an emergency... No, not that I know of... Blood type? Um... DEA 6, I think... Yes... Thank you so much. I'll be there as fast as I can." She pulls the phone away from her ear and checks something on the screen. "We have to go to my apartment first. I'm in Portland Towers."

"On 21st?"

She nods and I sense a bit of tension, like she's embarrassed to live in a building mostly inhabited by college students. She probably imagines I live in a nice house with my wife and kids and maybe even a few pets. She doesn't know that Tessa and I live in a generic two-bedroom apartment downtown and we have no children.

We make it to her building in seven minutes and I find myself getting nervous. How far do I take this act of kindness? Do I go inside? Do I help take her dog to the vet? The conversation she had with her mom a few minutes ago implied she has a car of her own, but she opted to ride her bike to work today. Technically, she no longer needs my help, but I have no idea how big her dog is. He could be a teacup poodle or a huge mastiff, in which case she definitely needs my help getting the dog into the car.

I park in a fifteen-minute loading zone right in front of the thirteen-story apartment building and kill the engine. I throw open my car door to follow her inside, but she stops me before she gets out of the car.

"What are you doing?" she asks, her voice still taut with tension. "I have a car. I'm fine. You need to go back to your meeting."

"I can help you carry the dog down, then I'll take off."

She hesitates for a moment, then she nods. "Okay. Thanks."

Following her into the elevator, I hold my breath as she presses the button for the eighth floor. Just walking behind her, I've gotten small whiffs of her hair. But I know the close quarters in the elevator will only amplify that. And I don't want her to know how crazy that scent is making me.

We stand side by side in total silence as the elevator ascends. The fingers on my right hand tingle, as if my skin can sense she's near. Then I realize it's probably because I'm holding my breath. Slowly, I breathe in, catching a strong whiff of vanilla that sends my heart racing. I clench my fist to keep from reaching out to touch her.

She glances down at my hand as she sees the slight movement from the corner of her eye. I relax my hand again so she doesn't think being this close to her is making me tense, but I don't believe for a second I can fool her.

She steps forward, closer to the elevator doors, putting more distance between us. A soft buzzing noise breaks through the silence just as the elevator doors slide open. She holds the phone to her ear as we exit onto the eighth floor.

"What's wrong?" she says, her eyebrows furrowed with worry, then her lips curl into an absolutely beautiful smile. "Oh, thank God… Yes, we just got here. I'll be right in." Holding the phone to her chest, she lets out a sigh of relief. "He's awake."

"That's great news."

She stops in front of apartment 811 and looks up at me. "I guess you can go."

"You're not still taking him to the vet?"

"Well, it's not an emergency anymore. I'll just have my mom take him in my car. She can walk him down now that he's awake."

My heart clenches as I realize I'm no longer needed. "Of course. So, you're okay?"

What a stupid loaded question.

She shrugs as she reaches for the doorknob. "As good as I can be," she replies, then suddenly she wraps her arms around my waist. "Thanks for the ride."

The smell of her hair hits me like a knife in the chest and I hold my breath to keep myself from completely inhaling her. I pat her on the back and she chuckles as she lets me go.

"Good luck with your pitch," she says, never looking back as she disappears into the apartment.

Jesus fucking Christ. I'm in deep shit here. I can't go back to the store for that meeting. There's no way I'll be able to work with Rory on a regular basis. If we open that wine bar, I'll have to check in at least once a week, probably more like two to three times a week.

I won't survive seeing her that often. I've barely survived the past five years.

But I can't throw away a multimillion-dollar joint venture contract. There's too much competition in the craft beer market these days. I need to take whatever bones are thrown my way.

I just wish I knew if Rory were *truly* okay. I can put myself through the agony of seeing her on a regular basis if I know it won't affect her. The last thing I want to do is make her work situation unbearable. She doesn't deserve that after what I did to her.

I MANAGED TO avoid bumping into Rory on the way out of the meeting at Zuckers by leaving the shop while she was busy with a customer. The pitch meeting with Jamie went well. When she heard why I stepped out earlier, she was quite impressed with my kindness toward the staff. I considered telling her that Rory is far from just a staff member to me, but I opted against it. If Rory wants her boss to know about our past, she should be the one to tell her.

As I drive away from Zucker's market, I think of going back to the brewery to see how Dean, our production manager, is coming along with the new winter lager. We've been brewing it in small batches in the pilot brewing system since January, and it won a gold medal at the Portland International Beer Festival last week. But today we're brewing the first large-scale production batch. Scaling up can be a bit tricky, but I'm confident Dean can handle everything on his own.

This batch of winter lager won't be ready for another twenty-three days. And if this deal with Zucker's goes through, it will be on tap at the new wine bar just in time for the holidays. I can relax tonight knowing I've done all I can today. Right now, I need to get home and see Tessa. I know that once I see her face, I'll know what I have to do.

I park the truck in the underground lot, then I head for the elevator. I pass the dog grooming station on the way, which Tessa always complains about. She thinks it's nice that the complex was built with the needs of pet owners in mind, but she thinks the wet-dog smell seeps into the underground parking structure and "infringes" on the other residents. Yet, as I breathe in the barnyard scent of freshly washed canine, all I can think of is what it would be like to help Rory give her dog a bath in there, suds flying everywhere, laughter echoing off the concrete walls.

I shake my head, trying to clear these dangerous thoughts as I enter the elevator. The doors are almost closed when someone sticks their arm through the gap. The doors slide open again and in walks Kendra Gris, our neighbor from across the hall and Tessa's new best friend. Kendra's a stay-at-home mom with an eight-month-old baby boy, Trucker. I'm not one to speak ill of a child, but I will say that Kendra and her husband, Aaron, really screwed their kid with a name like Trucker Gris.

"Hey, Kendra," I mutter, trying not to sound too annoyed.

She flashes me a tight-lipped smile as she pushes the stroller into the elevator then glances at the panel to make sure I've pressed the button for the third floor. She sighs as she flips her dark hair over her shoulder.

"Hey, Hugh."

I think back to the moment in Jamie's office earlier when Rory asked if she should call me Hugh or Houston. After five years, she still remembered that I prefer Houston, but this woman who sees me almost every day still insists on calling me Hugh.

"You're awfully quiet," Kendra remarks as the elevator doors open. "Bad day at the brewery?"

I exit right behind her as she pushes the stroller

36

down the hall. "It's been a long day."

"It's two o'clock," she sneers when she reaches her door. "Maybe you just need a few cold ones."

She pushes open the door with her back and pulls the stroller in backward, all the while flashing me a condescending smile. Kendra has told Tessa on more than one occasion that I drink too much. I don't.

I drink two, maybe three, beers a night to unwind after work. Sometimes when we're testing a new recipe, I'll drink too much, but I never get so drunk I black out or lose time. Beer is my life. I'm supposed to be a connoisseur. It's my job.

I enter the apartment and Tessa is sitting at the kitchen table with her computer. Her eyes widen when she looks up and sees me in the doorway. She deftly closes the laptop as she rises from the chair.

"Hey, I didn't expect you back so soon. Is something wrong?"

I shake my head as I drop my keys into the glass bowl on top of the table constructed out of salvaged Brazilian pine. "Everything's fine. I think the pitch went well. I'm… optimistic."

"That's great!" she replies, pulling her straight blonde hair into a ponytail at her nape as she walks toward me. "Why don't you look happy?"

"I am happy." I force a smile as I head for the refrigerator to grab a beer.

"Houston, it's two o'clock."

I glance at the beer in my hand then back at her. "Does it matter what time of day it is?"

"I'm not talking about the beer. I was just wondering why you're home so early on a Wednesday."

I can't tell her that I ran into my ex-girlfriend today and how the wall I'd built around my memories of Rory was knocked down in an instant. I can't tell her that I'm home early today because I didn't trust myself to be anywhere but here right now. I can't tell her that I hoped the sight of her would remind me of all the reasons I can't be with Rory.

Being married means having someone, just one person, who knows everything about you. Someone you can share everything with, even the ugly bits of your soul you'd rather sweep under the carpet and completely forget about. But Tessa doesn't know anything about Rory. That time of my life is a discussion I hoped I would never need to have with her.

"I told you. The meeting went well, so I just decided to take the rest of the day off. I wanted to see you."

I set the cold beer on the marble countertop, then I grab her waist and pull her body flush against mine. Gazing into her blue eyes for a moment, I will myself not to compare her to Rory, but it's difficult. Her sharp hip bones are pressed against me and I can't help but remember how much I loved the softness of Rory's body.

Leaning forward, I take her earlobe into my mouth.

Her breathing quickens as I trace the tip of my tongue inside the shell of her ear. Her hair smells like the lavender-mint shampoo we share and I inhale deeply to rid myself of the memory of Rory's hair, the way it smelled like vanilla frosting.

"Houston," she breathes, her fingers curling tightly around my biceps. "I... I have an appointment."

She pushes me back and her face is flushed as she opens a drawer and takes out a bottle opener. "I didn't know you were coming home early. I booked a hair appointment for this afternoon."

She pops the top off the bottle of beer I set down on the counter a few seconds ago, then she hands it to me.

I wish I could say that this is the first time Tessa has rejected my sexual advances, but that would be a lie. Any married couple will tell you that these kinds of things just don't always line up. Sometimes she has an appointment. Sometimes I have to get to work for an important meeting. Sometimes one of us is just not in the mood. But it's not the response I was hoping for. I wanted to lose myself in her today. Maybe even go for an all-nighter.

"You have a good time, baby."

She laughs nervously. "A good time at the hair salon?"

Before she can say anything else, I kiss her. Hard. Tangling my fingers in her hair, I thrust my tongue inside her mouth. She whimpers as she clutches the front of my

39

T-shirt. We move in unison and I'm reminded of the first time I met Tessa, at a beer festival three years ago.

She was wearing a floral crown on her head and totally blasted on free beer when she showed up at our booth. I probably could have taken her home with me and fucked her once then never called her again. It was what I had done for two years and it had worked just fine. But something she said changed my mind about using her.

She sampled our pale ale, then she looked me in the eye and said, *You look like my brother... He's dead.*

She cackled loudly at this proclamation and spilled the rest of the beer sample on her chest. Then she looked up at me again and her eyes swelled with tears. She apologized as her friend pulled her away from our booth, but I knew then that I wanted to know her.

I pull away, placing a soft kiss on her cheekbone before I whisper in her ear. "Hurry home. I don't think this beer is gonna quench my thirst tonight."

She nods as she reaches for her purse in a daze. "I'll be back soon."

As the door closes behind her, my eyes are drawn to the laptop on the table. Tessa never brings the laptop out here while I'm home. She says she doesn't like having electronic devices between us. So one of our unofficial wedding vows is to leave all electronic devices, other than cell phones, in the office. That way when we're home together we give each other our undivided attention.

I guess it's not a big deal if she brings the laptop out here while I'm at work. I take a seat on the sofa, but my gaze is still drawn to the table. Was it my imagination or was she nervous when I walked in at two o'clock?

No, that's just my own guilty conscience making me paranoid.

I stare at the laptop and for a brief moment consider opening it up to see what she was doing, but that would be a gross invasion of her privacy. Tessa is allowed to have her own personal space where I don't intrude.

And so am I.

Rory

Five years ago, May 28th

I SLIDE THE dollar bill into the vending machine on the first floor of the sociology building and, once again, it spits it back out.

"Piece of shit."

I smack the front of the machine as if this will make me feel better. I'm still thirsty as hell. Stuffing the dollar into my jeans pocket, my fingers bump into the new cell phone Houston gave me yesterday. The least romantic gift I expected to get, especially since I wasn't even expecting a gift. He's the one graduating next week and I still haven't decided what I want to get him.

I'm sure he would gladly accept a blow job as a graduation gift, but I had hoped we could do something

42

a normal couple would do. Maybe a private dinner or even just a weekend alone without a dozen frat guys spilling beer all over our carpet. Actually, I'd settle for just a decent truthful conversation.

For more than a month, Houston has dodged my questions about his plans for the summer. He's graduating with a degree in business. He got accepted to the UO School of Law, but I have a feeling he's not going to stay here. I'm not sure I understand throwing away that kind of opportunity. I'm also not sure I wouldn't do the same. Not a day goes by that I don't wish I could quit school, move somewhere no one knows me, and start over.

Houston pretty much told me he wanted the same, though he was rip-roaring drunk when he confided in me two weeks ago. I'm still not sure I believe that he was too drunk to know what he was saying.

Silver brushstrokes of moonlight painted across his muscular shoulders as he brushed the backs of his fingers across my cheekbone and looked me square in the eye. "Let's go. Let's get out of here."

His lips swept softly over mine as he leaned closer. I could smell the sweet ethanol fragrance of too much beer on his breath, but he could probably smell it on mine too. He slipped his knee between my legs as he slid closer to me, until his body was flush against my right side and his growing erection was prodding my hip.

"Go where?" Six months together and I still got

breathless whenever he was this close.

He kissed my jaw and nuzzled his face into the curve of my neck. "I don't know. South America. Indonesia. Anywhere. As long as it's just you and me and no one knows where we went. Let's do it."

"We can *do it* here," I replied with a soft chuckle.

He didn't laugh at my joke as he laid a tender kiss on the corner of my mouth. "Rory, we can fuck each other into submission anywhere." His hand slid behind my neck, lifting it so my head tilted back, so he could suck on the hollow of my throat. "But we can never be together here."

My heart stopped. "What are you talking about? We *are* together here."

He chuckled and the sound made my skin prickle with goose bumps. "I'm kidding. I'm just drunk." He climbed on top of me, lifting my leg so I could feel the tip of his solid erection pressed against my panties. "I love you, baby."

Then he kissed me and I forgot about that conversation and haven't thought about it since. Until this morning when I visited the university health center.

How am I going to tell him I'm pregnant? I'm pretty sure Houston wants a child as much as I do, which is *not at all*. This is not the kind of graduation gift I wanted to give him.

Maybe I should just get it taken care of without him. If I tell him, he might think I'm trying to imply that we should keep it. Or worse, he might think I'm trying to ask him to commit.

I know he likes to talk about the future and how we're going to get married after I graduate in three years, but I don't like to think that far ahead. Hallie had her whole life planned out and it didn't work out very well for her.

I love Houston. And I know he loves me and he would support me if I told him I wanted to terminate the pregnancy, but part of me is terrified of changing anything between us right now. We already have too much change to deal with this summer with him graduating and possibly moving two hours away to Portland, if he decides not to go to law school. I'm not sure our relationship could survive this.

Sometimes I wonder if our relationship is even real.

Hallie and I became best friends on the first day of sixth grade when the teacher sat us next to each other and we both discovered we were obsessed with Blink 182. She invited me over to her house after school that day so we could burn some songs onto a USB drive, and that's when I fell in love with Houston. I was eleven and he was fourteen, but in my warped prepubescent mind I was already concocting fantasies of us married with three children.

It's weird how our fantasies change as we mature. Now, I'd be happy just to *know* Houston after I graduate. Our connection is tenuous at best, no matter how many times he tells me he loves me and that we're going to spend the rest of our lives together. We're connected by a million fragile filaments, memories we've tried our hardest to pretend aren't there.

I once made the mistake of asking Houston if he remembered Hallie's favorite song.

His response: *I'm sure I'll completely forget after this fifth beer.*

We're not allowed to talk about the past in Houston's apartment. I sometimes wonder if it's this mutual desire to forget that brought us together or if he genuinely wanted to protect me when he asked me to move in with him six months ago. I could have moved in with Houston and kept to myself. I could have moved into another dorm. Or I could have opted not to move out of my old dorm at all. But I wanted to escape the memories as much as he did. I would have accepted a sleeping bag under a bridge at that point, anything not to have to enter that dorm ever again.

Instead, I moved in with Houston the same day he offered, and we slept together that first night. After seven years of pining for him, I convinced myself it was natural. We were meant to be together. It was okay to give myself to him so willingly.

I think I would have believed that even if we weren't brought together by tragedy. I was always ready to belong to Houston. But I was not ready for what came after.

I make it back to our off-campus apartment a few minutes after three and I'm not surprised to find I'm alone. Houston doesn't get home until a quarter after four on Wednesdays. I bought a couple of at-home pregnancy tests on the way home, just to make sure there wasn't a mix-up with my specimen at the health center. Five minutes later, I'm confused. The test is negative.

I take another brand of test and the results are positive. Now I'm even more confused. I lift the package off the bathroom counter to read the instructions again. I'm so lost in the small type, I don't notice when Houston walks in.

"What's that?"

I drop the box in the sink and let out a sharp yelp. "Jesus Christ, Houston. You scared the shit out of me. You're home early." I reach for the box, but he beats me to it. "Give me that."

His eyes widen as he holds the box up so I can't reach it. "A pregnancy test? Are you pregnant?"

"No! I mean, I don't know."

"I thought you were on the pill," he counters, but I don't appreciate the accusatory tone.

"I am! But it's not 100% effective, especially when consumed with alcohol."

He laughs. "Oh, so it's *my* fault you drink so much?"

"What? I don't drink that much!" I shout. "You drink more than I do."

"Did you do this on purpose?"

I stare into his blue eyes, unable to hide the anger boiling inside me. "Fuck you."

I push past him, but he grabs my wrist before I can leave the bathroom. "I'm sorry. That was a stupid thing to say."

I shake my arm free and head for the kitchen.

"Rory, I said I'm sorry. I didn't mean it. I know you wouldn't do something like that."

He follows me into the kitchen and pins me against the counter as I search for my car keys in my purse.

"Stop it, Houston."

"Are you pregnant or not?"

"Why do you care? I'm not keeping it."

He grabs my waist and turns me around roughly. "Are you saying I don't have a fucking choice?"

I lay my hands flat against his solid chest and try to push him back, but he doesn't move. "Get off me."

"Answer the question, Rory. Are you pregnant?"

"I don't know." I twist my body and duck under his arm to get away from him, then I head for the bedroom, where I left my backpack.

He follows so close behind me I can feel the heat of his body radiating on my shoulders. "What did the test say?"

"It was negative."

"So you're *not* pregnant?"

I grab the backpack on the bed and pull it upright so I can unzip the top. "I took three tests today. Two in the bathroom and one at the health center this morning... Two out of three were positive."

I pull my laptop out of the backpack and he takes it from me, flinging it onto the bed. "You're pregnant."

This time it's not a question. And it makes me sick to my stomach because I know it's true.

"I'm sorry," I whisper, staring at his chest as I wipe away the tears. "I don't know how this happened."

He grabs my face and tilts my head back so I can see the tears in his eyes. He doesn't speak for maybe a minute or two, but it feels like an eternity.

"We can do this."

"Do what?"

His arms envelop me, crushing me against him so tightly I feel as if my shoulders may dislocate. "We'll have the baby. We can't get rid of it... It's... This can't be a mistake."

My face is pressed against the solid warmth of his chest, so close I can hear his heartbeat, slow and steady. He's serious.

Houston

Five years ago, May 28th

I CAN'T TELL Rory the truth, that I'm no more ready to
have a baby than she is. But this realization that she's
pregnant has flipped a switch in me. It's as if everything
I've fucked up over the past six months has faded away
and I can finally see clearly. This is the opportunity I've
been waiting for. This is going to make all the lies and
the guilt worth it.

I kiss the top of her head and she sobs into my T-
shirt. "Hey," I whisper in her ear. "I know you're scared,
but I think I know how to fix that."

She swipes the back of her hand across her nose and
I can't help but smile. I grab the back of her neck with
one hand and with the other hand I pull up the bottom

of my T-shirt to wipe her nose.

She laughs as she pushes me away. "What are you *doing*?"

I chuckle as I grab her face so she can't get away. "Come here, Scar. Let me wipe your snot."

"Ew! Stop it!" she protests, giggling hysterically as I try to wrangle her in.

She loves it when I call her Scar. It's short for Scarlet, for her red hair, but also because sometimes she's as mean as Scar from *The Lion King*.

"See, I'll make an excellent father. I've watched *The Lion King* and I know how to wipe snot. You don't have to be afraid."

"Shut up." This takes some of the fight out of her, but she's still smiling uncontrollably as I pull her close. "Stop trying to make me laugh. This is serious."

I kiss the tip of her nose and wrap my arms around her shoulders. One of the things I love the most about her is that, at five-foot-four, she's twelve inches shorter than I am. I just want to tuck her in my pocket and keep her with me everywhere I go.

Plus, it makes for great wall sex.

"I know this is serious, which is exactly why I'm trying to make you laugh. That's the only way we'll get through this."

Her arms loosen around my waist and she looks up at me with those round hazel eyes that have never seen the real me. "What do you mean by 'That's the only way we'll get through this'? How are we going to get through this?"

I know there's only one correct response to this question, but I don't know if I can bring myself to say it. Once I say the words, there's no taking them back. I'll have to back up those words with actions, because there's no other alternative. Not for me.

I consider leaving the room to get the ring I have hidden underneath our bed, but I'm afraid I'll talk myself out of it in the short time it will take to do that. I've already spent the past couple of weeks since I got her the ring trying to talk myself out of it, convincing myself that nothing good will come of it.

That's it. I'm doing it.

I take both her hands in mine, then I step back and look her in the eye as I get down on one knee. Her eyes widen and her whole body begins to tremble. She knows what I'm about to do.

"Rory—Aurora—well, I—I don't know the proper way to do this."

"Houston, please, you don't have—"

"No, just listen."

Rory knows there's no use trying to talk me out of doing something once my mind is set. But is my mind really set on this?

She smiles as she kneels before me. "Then I'm coming down here with you."

"Get up, baby. It's *my* turn to get on my knees."

She smacks my arm and I smile as I try to help her back to her feet, but she refuses to stand. "I'm not getting up. If we're doing this, we're doing it together… from beginning to end."

Her words make my stomach vault into my throat. I can't do this. If I marry Rory, then I'll have no choice but to tell her the truth. And I love her too much to do that.

"Get up, Rory. We can't do this."

"What?"

I stand up and hold my hand out to help her up, trying not to look her in the eye so I can't see the hurt. She stands up and I don't see her hand coming at me until it's too late. Her palm lands hard on my jaw, making a popping sound so loud I think she may have broken something.

"What the fuck?" I roar at her, rubbing my face to soothe the burn.

"I knew you were an asshole, but I never thought you'd do something like this. You just made a fool out of me. What kind of person stops proposing in the middle of the proposal? An asshole."

"Getting married isn't the answer."

She storms off toward the bedroom and stuffs her laptop back into her backpack. "I'm leaving."

"Rory, please, just stay. We need to talk about this."

"I don't want to talk to you." She pulls the backpack on and rounds on me. "I don't want to see you. I don't want to know you."

My chest aches as I finally grasp that this is it. This is the solution I've been waiting for since the day I realized inviting Rory to live with me was a huge mistake. Though I know this is what I've been waiting for, there is no sense of relief and it doesn't hurt any less. On the contrary, it fucking kills.

"You don't have to leave. The rent is paid up until the end of June. That's thirty-four days. You can keep the apartment and I'll stay with Troy until I find another place."

She laughs as she wipes tears from her cheeks. "I knew this would be your reaction. I knew the minute they told me the test was positive that this would happen. You're so fucking predictable it's disgusting."

I know I deserve this, but I wish I could grab her and shake her and force her to see the truth. The truth that has been right under her nose for six months. The truth that I have so foolishly hidden from her when I should have told her everything from the beginning. Then I wouldn't feel like the past six months of my life were a lie.

I want to take her in my arms and apologize for not being a better man, but she needs a clean break. She doesn't need me begging for forgiveness and further confusing the situation. This is the end. It has to end now or it will only get worse before it ends later.

"What do you need?" I ask, breaking the heavy

silence.

She looks up at me, confused by this question.

"I mean, do you need money for the… procedure?" I clarify.

Her lips tremble as she presses them together and turns her head so she doesn't have to look at me. "I need you to get out."

"I don't want you to do this alone."

"Just get out," she whispers.

"Baby—I mean, *fuck*, Rory. Come on. You can't do this alone."

She steps around me. "Fine. I'll leave."

I grab her forearm to stop her. "No, I'll leave. You stay."

I can't allow her to leave this apartment. I don't know where she'll end up. She doesn't have any close friends anymore.

Striding past her, I turn around when I reach the doorway, marveling at the mess I've made. "You're staying. I'm leaving." I grab the doorframe for support as it hits me that I've just made the worst mistake of my life. "And I promise I won't bother you, but I need you to promise me something, too."

She stares at the carpet, unwilling to meet my gaze.

"Rory, please promise me you'll call if you need anything. Ever."

She steps backward and sits down on the edge of the bed, still refusing to look up at me. "Just get out."

Rory

August 15th

MY DOG HAS diabetes. I thought the vet was joking when he told me this. *My perfect Skippy can't have diabetes.* But he does. And he will need insulin injections for the rest of his life. My poor Skip.

After spending two nights in the animal hospital, and after waiting patiently for me to receive a thirty-minute lesson on how to test his blood glucose and give him an insulin shot, Skippy was ready to come home. The moment he climbs into my twelve-year-old Toyota, his tail wags relentlessly and he whines for me to open the window.

"Settle down, Skip. We'll be home soon."

I roll the passenger window all the way down and he

grins as he juts his head out. He closes his eyes, panting heavily as the sun warms his face. I love him so much. I don't know what I would have done if I'd lost him.

My phone vibrates in my pocket and I slip it out to check the number. I don't recognize it so I hit the red button to decline the call, then I drive home.

The streets of Portland are lively with the trappings of summer. Outdoor patios at cafés are bustling. Bicyclists swish by when I'm stopped in traffic. Protestors are picketing in their shorts and tank tops outside the Justice Center. The air blasting through my car window smells like hot concrete and there are few clouds in the sky, but the threat of rain is always present.

I moved to Portland after I graduated from UO. It seemed like the logical next step. I was born and raised in McMinnville, about an hour's drive from Portland. Even after the population doubled, McMinnville is still the kind of small town that is too spread out to have a true small-town feel. Don't get me wrong, everyone knows everyone's business in McMinnville, but there's still a disjointed quality to the town that never sat right with me. As if the town had been planned by someone with attachment issues.

Hallie and Houston moved to McMinnville the summer before we began middle school and Houston began high school. Looking back, it seemed like a logical time for them to move, I suppose. Their parents had just divorced and their mom, Ava, wanted to start fresh.

Their father had been having an affair for years and Ava couldn't seem to escape all the people who had kept it a secret from her.

This must have affected Houston, knowing that his father was the one who had betrayed his mother for so long and still *she* was the one who'd had to move away to escape the memories. I often wonder if Houston was cheating on me while we were together, which is why he insisted I keep the apartment out of some misplaced sense of guilt. So he wouldn't feel like a total bastard like his father. But I think the truth about why Houston left is much worse.

The truth is, Houston probably never loved me.

It took a near-miss with a wedding proposal to jolt the truth out of him. As painful as it is to know I spent so many years of my life loving someone who was incapable of loving me back, I'm still grateful for the months I spent curled up next to him, wrapped in his arms. Even if it was all a lie, those were still the best moments of my life.

Skippy and I are settled on the sofa, ready to spend Friday night catching up on the past few episodes of *The Good Wife*. I flinch a little when my phone buzzes. I snatch it off the coffee table and Skip and I both look at the screen. It's the same unknown number that called me earlier.

"Should I answer?" I ask the dog and he looks up at me, his brow furrowed, wondering when I'm going to make the stupid thing stop buzzing.

I sigh as I hit the green button. "Hello?"

"Rory, it's Houston. Do you have a minute?"

My first instinct is to hang up. I can't talk to Houston on the phone. He's married.

"Houston, what are you doing?" I whisper, as if his wife is sitting next to me. "You can't call me. How did you even get my number? Forget it. I don't care how you got it. Just don't call me."

The last thing I hear as I hang up is Houston calling my name. I stare at the phone for a second, expecting him to call back. Foolishly *wishing* he'd call back. Then I hug my knees to my chest as I wonder what he could have possibly been calling about.

Skip breaks me out of my trance by stuffing his snout under my armpit. I laugh as I push his head back. "Is that a hint? Are you saying I need a shower?"

I stretch my legs out and rest my feet on the coffee table so he can lay his head on my lap, then I turn on the TV and try not to think about Houston. But, at this point, trying not to think about him is like trying not to breathe.

After he drove me to my apartment two days ago, I was on high alert at the store. As I bagged groceries and punched in product codes, I'd glance over my shoulder at the sliding doors, watching the customers as they came and went. I don't know if I was more afraid or excited at the prospect of seeing him. All I know is that I didn't want to be caught unaware again. But he never came back to the store after his meeting with Jamie on Wednesday. And I've been too afraid to ask Jamie whether or not their meeting went well. I don't want to show too much interest in this wine bar project as I have no intention of telling Jamie that Houston and I have a past.

An hour later, I have no idea what happened in that episode of *The Good Wife*. I may as well just take a shower and go to bed. I clip on Skip's leash so I can take him outside to do his business before I give him his insulin. When I exit the front entrance of the apartment building, my stomach flips at the sight of a white SUV parked next to the curb.

An Asian woman climbs down from the passenger side and waves at the driver. I squint through the darkness and, through the glare on the windshield, I can barely make out another woman in the driver's seat. Letting out a soft sigh, I lead Skip around to the back of the building where there's a small greenway for him to do his duty.

I clean up after him with a biodegradable waste bag and toss the bag into the receptacle at the end of the greenway marked "Doggy Bags." I round the corner to the front of the building and the SUV is back. I never noticed how many people in this complex have white SUVs, though I suppose I'll probably start noticing them everywhere now. That's the way these things work. After

Houston and I broke up, my heart would stop every time I saw a gray Chevy truck.

Of course, I wasn't really afraid of running into him then. Houston had moved to Portland right after graduation, less than one week after we broke up. It was my memories of him I was afraid of.

"Rory."

I jump at the sound of his voice. Whipping my head around, I catch Houston entering the lobby behind me.

"You scared the hell out of me."

"Sorry," he says with a smile that's sexy enough to stop my heart.

My cheeks get hot and this makes me irrationally angry. "Go home, Houston."

"Nice to see you, too," he replies, following me to the elevator. "I need to talk to you. We need to talk."

I punch the elevator call button and look up at him. "We didn't speak for five years and we did just fine."

The elevator doors open and I roll my eyes as he steps in after me. I coil Skippy's leash around my hand to pull him closer. Houston smiles as the dog licks the back of his hand.

"Hey, buddy. You feeling better?" he says as he scratches Skip behind the ear.

Skip pulls on the leash as he tries to get closer to Houston, but I maintain a tight grip.

"You can't get to me through my dog."

"I'm not trying to get to you. I just need to talk."

He kneels down and laughs as Skippy laps at his jaw, and for a moment all I can remember is the raw feeling I used to get from hours of kissing Houston. He used to refer to his scruff as a "free exfoliating treatment." I turn away so I don't have to see Houston kneeling down before me, scratching Skippy's throat. So I don't have to wonder if that's what he looked like when he proposed to his wife, supplicating and still so damn happy.

I never understood the tradition of a man kneeling before a woman and begging her to marry him. Which is why I also got down on my knees when I thought Houston was going to propose to me. I wanted him to know he didn't need to beg me to be with him. I was already his.

Houston stands as the elevator doors slide open. "I need to talk to you about the work situation," he says as he follows me out. "I got the contract, but I want to make sure you're okay with this before I sign it."

"You want to know if I'll be okay working with you?"

I slide the key into the doorknob and Houston places his hand over mine to stop me from turning the knob. "I can't go in there with you. Please stay out here until we're done talking."

I shake his hand off and turn around to face him. "There's nothing to talk about. You have to sign the contract. The way I feel about working with you shouldn't matter."

"But it *does* matter. I don't want to upset you. You were there first."

I can't help but laugh. "So this is a territorial thing? You think because I was there first that I have some sort of right to keep you out?"

His left eyebrow shoots up the way it always does when he's confused, and it nearly renders me mute.

I shake my head to clear the momentary distraction. "Houston, if I didn't work there you wouldn't think twice about signing that contract. So that's what you should do. Just… please stop making this into something it isn't. We hardly know each other anymore, and that's the way it's going to stay."

He swallows hard as he lets this sink in. "I guess you're right. I'm sorry I bothered you. I only wanted to… Never mind. I'll get going. I have to get up early to go sign that contract. Not that you care."

He shakes his head in disappointment as he walks away and I'm glad I don't have anything solid in my hand other than Skippy's leash or I might throw it at the back of his head. So *I'm* the one who doesn't care? *Ugh*. Typical Houston and his endless psychological games.

Maybe I should have told him to walk away from the contract, but that would have meant admitting that he still has this much power over me. It also would have been the truth, and the truth has never gotten me into trouble. In fact, the truth is something my previous relationship with Houston was sorely lacking.

Nevertheless, I don't need to right the wrongs we made while we were together. I don't need to tell Houston that the sight of him makes my throat dry and my stomach flutter. He doesn't need to know that I still go to sleep with scenes from our life together playing on repeat in my mind. Or that sometimes I wake with his name tumbling from my lips, the remnants of dreams where he never left and nightmares where he hovers just out of reach.

Before Wednesday, the last time I had seen Houston was the day after he met me at the Planned Parenthood clinic. I didn't ask him to come, and I don't know how he found out the date and time of my appointment, but he was there when we pulled into the parking lot. Lisa, a girl from my Social Inequality class whom I'd had coffee with a couple of times, had graciously agreed to take me to the clinic. The moment we pulled into the lot and I saw Houston leaning against his truck, I knew I had to send Lisa home. He would insist on driving me back to the apartment after the procedure, to watch over me.

It was the last thing I wanted, to have Houston doting over me after terminating the pregnancy. But it was also the only thing I wanted. It was as if he was performing the last rites on our dead relationship.

It took me a while to wake up after the D&C. I didn't want to be conscious while they did it, so I opted for a sedative in addition to the local anesthesia. The nurse pushed me out the back door of the clinic in a wheelchair all the way to Houston's truck. He scooped me up out of the chair and gently placed me in the passenger seat as if I weighed nothing. I closed my eyes and pretended not to feel it when he kissed my forehead before turning the key in the ignition.

I head into my apartment and hang up Skippy's leash inside the coat closet. As I'm getting undressed to get into the shower, my phone lets out a short buzz. I'm almost afraid to look at it, but it could be my mom. She loves texting me. She thinks it makes her a "hipster."

> **Houston:** *I promise this is the last message you'll get from me. I just want to thank you for not making this more difficult when you have every right to.*

I sit on the edge of my bed and stare at the words on the screen in a daze. Is this how mature adults behave when they're confronted with the painful memories of a past relationship? Should I be trying to sabotage his contract? Is that what he expected me to do?

I take a deep breath and let it out as I begin typing my response.

> **Me:** *I'm not trying to make this less difficult. I'm trying not to fall. I'd appreciate it if you could respect that.*

My index finger hovers over the send button. As

much as I want to be honest with Houston, I know I can't send this message. The window of opportunity for honesty closed the minute he got married, whenever that was.

I delete the words I typed without sending the message, then I delete Houston's text message to me and his phone number from my call history. *Hey, Houston, how does it feel to be erased? Again.*

Houston

MY ATTEMPT TO clarify my position with Rory failed spectacularly. And I can't say I'm surprised. Rory always had a way of calling me out on my bullshit, even if she was completely oblivious to the biggest lie I ever told her. Actually, it was the biggest lie I've ever told anyone.

The truth: Hallie left a suicide note. The bigger truth: That note is the reason Rory and I got together. And the biggest, most despicable truth of all is the one conveyed to me, and only me, in that suicide note. Hallie's last words.

I know most people wouldn't understand it. And most people would be absolutely disgusted with me for what I did to Rory. But the truth is that I allowed my loyalty to my sister to eclipse my loyalty to the only girl I've ever loved. The only girl I may *ever* love.

So when I come out of the bathroom with sweat beaded on my chest and a towel wrapped around my waist, I'm a little disgusted—not just with myself—to see Tessa checking me out. She's lying on the bed with her phone hovering above her. When we first started living together, I loved watching her in this position because inevitably she would drop the phone on her forehead. It's one of her cuter quirks.

Today, I find myself wishing she'd drop the phone on her face just so she'll stop staring at my body. I'm a bad person. I know that. But I can't help wishing it were Rory lying in my bed.

"Hey, handsome," Tessa purrs as I open the top drawer of our dresser and pull out a pair of gray boxer briefs.

"Hey, baby."

I shed the towel and toss it onto the chair by the window, then I pull on the boxers.

"I don't think you're gonna need those tonight."

I turn around and she's casting her best come-hither expression in my direction. I try to see Tessa the way I saw her three days ago, as my hot, blonde twenty-six-year-old wife. The woman who gave me a distraction from the painful memories when I thought they would consume me. But all I see when I look at her is two words flashing in bold letters: NOT RORY.

I smile at Tessa and squint my eyes a bit to return her sexy glare. "Is that an invitation?"

The words feel wrong and misshapen in my mouth. Like I'm rehearsing lines from a movie script.

"Do you *need* an invitation?"

She lays her phone down on the nightstand and I know there's no getting out of this. A man can't refuse sex the way a woman can. And, of course, I am only a man. I also have needs. I can't save myself for Rory when there's probably zero chance she'll ever take me back.

I push down my boxers and kick them off as I climb onto the bed. She giggles as I slide between her legs, placing my hands on each side of her head as I lean down to kiss her. She tastes like toothpaste and betrayal.

I reach down and hastily pull off her panties and she yelps. "Hey! Take it easy, tiger."

Sliding my hand behind her nape, I pull her head to the side, exposing her neck, then I suck hard on her pale flesh. She pushes me back.

"What are you doing? You're gonna leave a mark."

"Sorry." I push up on my hands and look down at her, trying to convey the hunger in my eyes. "Turn around."

She gazes into my eyes, trying to figure out what's going on with me, but she decides not to question it. She flips over onto her belly and I wrap my arm around her middle to lift her up onto all fours.

Doggy-style is a primal sex position. It's the position we perfected as apes and we carried it with us when we became human. I think this is probably why so many women are opposed to it. When sex became less about procreation and more about emotional connection, women lost their love for doggy-style.

Now women want to look into your eyes when you come. They want to imprint the image of their face in your memory at that climactic moment so you associate their visage with your ultimate desire. It's all a psychological game.

Tessa doesn't like doggy-style, but she tolerates it because I like it. The worst part is that she'd be right in assuming I'm imagining someone else when I fuck her from behind.

I slide the tip of my cock over her clit a few times to get her extra wet, then I glide into her. "Fuck," I hiss through gritted teeth.

I close my eyes and try not to picture Rory as I slide in and out of Tessa, but all I can think is how Rory's cheeks were softer and creamier and how much I'd rather be buried inside her right now. I have to stop this. I'm coveting that which I cannot have.

I open my eyes and focus on Tessa's body. I lean forward, sliding my hand under her tank top to grab her breast. She looks back at me over her shoulder and I feel myself getting strangely annoyed by the look on her face. Letting go of her breast, I stand up straight again and grab her hips to drive her harder. But she keeps looking at me.

I close my eyes and force myself to think of anything other than Rory. First, I think about work, and visions of brew tanks and bags of barley and hops flash in my mind. Then I think of my office and suddenly I remember that box I have hidden in the closet of my office.

I open my eyes to clear away this memory. My thrusts are slow and deliberate as I try to focus on anything but Rory and her soft, pliant body laid out beneath me. I try not to think of the perfect fit of my mouth on hers. Or the time we became parents for two seconds. Then it was over.

When I took Rory home, after she had the abortion, I waited until she had slept off the sedative. Then I waited until she had washed up, pretending not to hear the aching song of her cries in the shower. Then I waited some more, until she had eaten solid food and fallen asleep. Then I left.

I've been waiting five years to tell her the truth. The truth about Hallie. The truth about why we were together. And, most of all, the truth about how I've never stopped loving her. I'm tired of waiting.

I pound Tessa from behind, completely oblivious as to whether or not she's actually enjoying herself. All I can see and hear over my blinding memories of Rory is the vague curve of Tessa's hips and the faint sound of her moans. Whether those are cries of pain or ecstasy I don't know.

Because even if those are cries of ecstasy, Tessa will still find a way to complain. No matter how many times I fuck her senseless. No matter how many times I make her come so hard she cries real tears. No matter what, it will never be enough unless I fuck her with the intention of making a baby.

I told Tessa from the beginning of our relationship that I don't want children. But she was undeterred. She probably convinced herself that she could change my mind.

I will never change my mind about wanting children with Tessa. And the reason is simple: I don't want to have to choose.

If Rory ever wanted to give me a second chance, I wouldn't want to choose between her and my children. And I know it's crazy to risk losing my wife over something that may never happen—will almost *certainly* never happen—but I can't bring children into my life when I'm still living a lie.

My cock twitches and I pull out of Tessa. She waits as I come on her ass, then I grab a tissue off the nightstand and quickly wipe it off. She turns over and narrows her eyes at me. I know what she's thinking.

I always come inside her. She has an IUD implanted in her uterus, which means she has less than half of one percent chance of getting pregnant. Not a single pregnancy has been reported with the use of this particular IUD, so I've always been quite happy to release my load inside her. But I can't bring myself to do it tonight.

Rory was on birth control when she got pregnant. And I know a .05 percent failure rate on this IUD means it's basically impossible for the same thing to happen with Tessa, but I can't take the chance anymore. I *won't* take the chance anymore.

"Why did you do that?" she asks as I climb off the bed and head for the door.

"Do what?"

"You know what."

I keep walking into the corridor. "I don't know what you're talking about."

I make it to the kitchen and manage to pour myself a glass of cold water before she catches up with me. Her panties are back on and her face is contorted in disbelief.

"Are you fucking someone else?"

This wouldn't be the first time Tessa has accused me of having an affair with absolutely no evidence. I'm pretty certain she does it just to remind me how much I don't want to end up like my father. But this tactic isn't going to work with me tonight.

"What?" I reply calmly, placing the empty glass in the sink.

"You heard me. Are you fucking someone else?"

I let out a soft chuckle as I shake my head. "I didn't

come inside you, so now I'm having a fucking affair? What if I happened to read an article on the ineffectiveness of IUDs today? Nope. Right away you jump to the worst fucking conclusion."

She gets in my face. "*Did* you read an article on IUDs today?"

I roll my eyes as I try to step around her, but she blocks my path. "No. No, I didn't. Are you happy now?"

Her gaze falls to my chest and she swallows hard. "I think I'm gonna be sick."

I sigh as I grab her face. "Tessa, I'm not cheating on you. I'm just... I'm sorry."

She looks into my eyes. "Sorry for what?"

What am I supposed to say? *I'm sorry for not coming inside you... I'm sorry for fantasizing about someone else while I was fucking you.*

I'm sorry I never loved you.

"I'm sorry for being in a shitty mood. It's not your fault. I'm just stressed about this new contract." I pull her face to mine and kiss her softly on the lips. "I love you. Come to bed and we'll do it right this time."

She lets out a soft sigh as her shoulders slump with defeat. She nods and I take her hand as I lead her back to the bedroom for round two. I'll let her win this one.

Rory

August 16th

DURING MY SENIOR year at UO, I worked as a fiction editor for *Unbound*, the university's literary arts magazine. It was my job to work with submitting writers to get their pieces ready for publication. Though, since I was the new kid on the editing team, most of my time was spent reading through submissions, some of them terrible enough to make my eyes bleed. But every once in a while a submission would come through with the kind of prose that made my insides ache with envy. Sometimes, it wasn't just words arranged on a page. Sometimes, I would open up a submission and smell the fumes of gasoline and smoke after a furious car crash; hear the echoing cries of a sick child in my mind long after their passing; feel the searing tendrils of lust curling inside me from a passionate affair. Sometimes, I would get a sensory experience.

It was my semester working for *Unbound* that inspired me to write my *own* sensory experience. At first, I tried writing something completely fictional, a story about a detective who's investigating a murder where her longtime lover is implicated. But I couldn't seem to rein in the story. There were too many plot lines and plot holes, and none of it really made sense. Then I decided I would write a children's book. It was safe. But I quickly realized it was *too* safe. I needed something a bit more challenging.

Then it dawned on me that the one project I was avoiding would probably be the most challenging project of them all: the story of us.

Over the past two years, I've written 227 pages in the as-yet-untitled story of Houston and me. But six weeks ago I reached the climax where everything falls apart and I can't bring myself to write anymore. My mind knows how the story ends, but my heart is demanding a rewrite.

My mom brings me a steaming mug of black coffee, setting it down on the table in front of me. "Shouldn't you be at work?" she asks, taking a seat at the other end of the sofa.

Skippy lies peacefully between us, having just ingested his morning ration of dog food and insulin.

"I switched with Kenny so I could stay home with

Skip today on his first day back from the vet. Right, Skippers?" I scratch his shoulder and he stretches his arms and legs out lazily.

My mom rolls her eyes as she brings her cup of tea to her lips, takes a slow sip, then sets the mug down on the coffee table. She flips back her shoulder-length prematurely gray hair and leans back. She's going to tell me what I *should* be doing today.

"You should be working on your book, not watching TV. Where's your ambition?"

I grab my cup of coffee off the table and take a sip, mentally cursing my mom for knowing how to make coffee better than I do. "My ambition, or lack thereof, has nothing to do with why I'm not writing."

"Are you stuck? Because you know I'd be glad to help you. Just give me a few pages and I'll tell you why you're stuck."

My mother taught high school English for twenty-five years, until she retired a little more than three years ago. My parents' divorce came about six months after Hallie died; just two weeks after Houston and I broke up. That was definitely the worst summer of my life. Then one year later, my mother retired. She declared her classroom days were over and she would be starting fresh, without my father.

I assumed this meant that she would finally write that novel she'd had kicking around inside her head for the past twenty-some years, but I was wrong. She's spent the past three years trying to live vicariously through me. She desperately wants *me* to write my novel, though she has no idea if it's actually any good, since I refuse to let her get anywhere near it with her English-teacher-eyes.

"I don't need you to look at it. It's not even edited. It's a first draft. I just need to put it in a drawer for a while. Come back to it with fresh eyes in a month or two."

My mother crosses one slender ankle over the other and purses her lips at me. "You're so afraid I'll hurt your feelings by insulting your writing. That actually hurts me, you know. I would never purposely tear apart your work."

Yeah, she would never *purposely* tear it apart. *Oops! What's this dangling participle here and that cardboard character there? And how about this misguided attempt at theme? Really, Rory, you call this fiction?* My mother is probably the perfect person to provide feedback on my novel, but she will never get her hands on it because it's too personal. I don't want her to know how deeply I fell.

"Fine. If you're not going to write, then you need to get up and get out of those lady boxer shorts. Go find yourself a man so you can wear *his* boxer shorts."

"Ew!" I shriek. "Don't talk to me about that kind of stuff."

"Oh, please, Rory. You're twenty-four years old. You can have an adult conversation. You can't keep denying yourself. We all have needs."

"Double-ew. Please don't talk to me about *needs*."

She glances around the living room as she slides my mug aside and sits on the coffee table in front of me. "Maybe you should make one of those online dating profiles. You're a beautiful girl, Rory." She smiles as she reaches forward and pets my hair. "You're smart. You're self-sufficient. You're healthy."

"And I'm purebred."

"Oh, Rory, stop making everything into a joke. Men will see it as a defense mechanism and they'll wonder what you're hiding."

"I'm hiding from men. Isn't that obvious?"

She sighs heavily as she lays her clasped hands in her lap.

"Okay, that's enough, Mom. If you want to make an online dating profile, make one for yourself. Leave me and my defense mechanisms out of it."

I stand from the sofa and scoop the coffee mug off the table to take it to the kitchen. I don't know why I'm taking it to the kitchen, other than I need an excuse to get away from my mother.

She calls out after me. "You know, you have more than one soul mate in this world, Rory." She pauses to let this sink in. "There really *are* plenty of fish in the sea."

"Yeah, and most of them are slimy eels or boring sand dollars," I shout back at her as I dump my coffee into the steel sink. "I want a smart, spunky dolphin. Is that too much to ask?"

A smart, spunky dolphin named Houston.

Just thinking these words makes me sick to my stomach.

My mom arrives in the kitchen with her tea mug. "A smart, spunky dolphin? Is that how you remember Houston? Because I remember him being an arrogant frat boy."

After five years of hearing these kinds of insults directed at Houston, it still makes me as angry as it did the first time. "This conversation is over."

She follows me out of the kitchen and I brace myself for more criticism as she trails behind me. "Rory, you don't need to be ashamed for loving Houston as he was, but it's been five years. You need to stop remembering him through the telescopic view of young love. You need to look at the big picture. At reality. And the reality is that he left you. He. Left. You."

"That's enough, Mom." I stop in the hallway and round on her. "That's. Enough."

Her eyebrows knit together as she nods. "I'm sorry. I just want you to be happy. You deserve to be happy again."

Why is everyone always trying to tell me what I deserve? My mom insists I deserve to be happy. Houston insists I deserve to decide whether or not he should sign a contract. It's as if everyone knows something about me that I don't know about myself.

I'm no more deserving of happiness than anyone

else. I'm just a screwed-up girl with a billion stories racing through my mind on any given day. And only one story I really want to tell.

Rory

MY NERVES ARE buzzing as I make my way through Zucker's icy warehouse. Taking a deep breath, I push through the swinging door and enter the store. Right away, I busy myself with tidying up a display of dried apple chips in the produce section. Then I keep my head down as I make my way to the cash register. I don't know if Houston is coming in today, but I know he came in yesterday to sign the contract, which is the real reason I switched shifts with Kenny.

Kenny and I are both working today and I breathe a sigh of relief when I see him standing behind register four. He's the only person in this store that I could *maybe* call my friend, though I've only hung out with him outside of work on one occasion. He's also the only person in this store I would trust to balance my cash drawer if I were to suddenly drop dead while ringing up a bottle of organic shampoo.

Kenny is ridiculously attractive and completely gay, so he's as safe as a children's book. But that doesn't stop him from flirting with me. I'm sure in his twisted twenty-two-year-old mind, I'm as safe as a children's book to him, because I'm hopelessly incapable of forming new attachments. He knows I won't misinterpret his flirtations.

"Hey, beautiful," Kenny says as I slide in behind register three.

Unlocking the drawer, I pull it out completely. Then I walk past Kenny's register toward the service register at the front of the store, where Jamie is on the phone. We exchange my empty drawer for the drawer she has waiting for me under the counter. Checking the amount on the register slip, I sign it and hand it back to her. She time-stamps the slip and tucks it beneath the money tray inside the service register.

Carrying my cash back to my station, I easily lose myself in the monotony of setting up my drawer. I don't notice there's someone at my register until I hear the unmistakable sound of a woman clearing her throat. Looking up, I want to say something, but I find myself stunned into silence. The girl at my register has the same straight, light-brown hair as Hallie. She's wearing a crooked smile as she tucks her hair behind her ear while holding out a pack of gum to me.

"Are you open?" she asks so softly I can barely hear her over the sound of Kenny's scanner beeping.

I nod hastily and turn back to my register to punch in my password. "Yeah, just a minute." The system takes a few seconds to log me in and I smile as I take the pack of gum from her to ring it up. "Do you want a bag?"

"No, thanks," she replies, taking the gum back and walking away, completely oblivious of her resemblance to my dead friend.

"Hey, sexy, can I trade you a ten for a roll of quarters?"

I look up and Kenny winks at me as he holds out a ten-dollar bill. I grab a roll of quarters out of the drawer and exchange it for the ten, then I turn back to the keypad in front of me, trying not to think about Hallie.

The one thought I couldn't escape after she committed suicide was the idea that I may never have truly known her. Hallie and I had both known of kids who had taken their lives and, at the time, we could see how it was inevitable. *Joe was always wearing black... Stacy never had any boyfriends... Paul was always playing those violent video games.* But in the end, it was my own best friend's death that stumped me. I didn't see it coming.

It didn't help that she didn't leave a note.

Closure is a weird word. It implies that something is closed. Finished. But how can you find closure when someone you love dies? They're already gone. The case is closed. There's nowhere to go from there.

There's no one to give you answers that make any sense. Which is why, after the shock of Hallie's death wore off, I became very angry with her. How could she leave me behind without any explanation? Did I not deserve to know her story?

There goes that word again: deserve.

I make it through the rest of the workday without any appearances from Houston. Kenny walks me out to the back of the store where my bike is parked.

"Want to go to Ración with us tonight? We have a reservation at eight, but someone in our party canceled. You know you want to come."

It's been about five months since I've taken Kenny up on one of his offers to get out of the house. I've been using the excuse of writing my book, but I can't really use that anymore since I haven't written a single word in six weeks.

I kneel down next to my bike to punch in the code on the padlock. "Who's going? I'm not going if Lina's there."

Lina is Kenny's bisexual friend who hit on me the last time I went to dinner with him and his crowd. She made some pretty crude remarks after I rejected her, too. I would have left the restaurant right then if it weren't for Heather, Kenny's straight friend who explained to me that Lina was going through a bad breakup. That was something I could relate to.

"Lina moved to Seattle with her new boyfriend months ago."

I climb onto my bike and nod. "Sure. I'll meet you there."

"Yay!" Kenny shouts as he throws his arms around me so suddenly I almost lose my balance. "I've missed hanging out with you."

I hug him back and refrain from reminding him that we've only hung out once before. "I've missed you, too."

He kisses my cheek as he lets me go. "What are you going to wear?"

I open my mouth to reply, but no words come out. My gaze is locked on a white SUV parked at the end of the service alley behind the market. I know it's just my mind playing tricks on me again, my subconscious fear of running into Houston.

Kenny follows the direction of my stare to the SUV. "Who's that?"

"No one."

The driver's side door opens and my breath hitches as Houston steps out. What is he doing here? Is he following me?

"Sure doesn't look like no one," Kenny says. "Looks like a very delicious someone."

I swallow hard and turn back to Kenny and throw my arms around him again. "I'll see you later."

He chuckles as he seizes the opportunity to squeeze

me firmly. "Oh, yeah, baby. You know how I like it. Hug me tighter."

I squeeze a little harder. "Is this tight enough?"

"No, harder!"

I laugh as I push him away. "Go home."

He kisses my forehead before he turns to walk away. "Don't stand me up, gorgeous."

I slide my helmet off the handlebars and try to pretend I don't notice Houston walking toward me.

"Hey," he says, his voice a bit breathy, as if he's nervous.

I look up and try to think of a response other than *Go home to your wife.* "Hey," I reply tersely.

Houston looks back over his shoulder at the corner of the building Kenny just disappeared behind. "Who was that?"

I should slip this helmet onto my head, ignoring his question as I ride off into the sunset. But I can't.

"Why does it matter?"

He smiles at my impertinence. "I guess it doesn't. Do you need a ride?"

I narrow my eyes at him in disbelief. "Are you seriously offering me a ride?"

The muscle in his jaw twitches. "Rory, I don't know what's going to happen when I come in here to oversee the setup of the bar, but I know that this"—he wags his finger to indicate the space between us—"can't continue. We can't work together with all this animosity."

"Why?"

His eyebrows furrow in confusion. "Because it's not healthy."

"Suddenly you're worried about maintaining a healthy relationship with me?"

He sighs as he looks down at the asphalt. "I deserve that."

"Look, Houston, if you want to maintain a healthy working relationship with me, I think the first part of that would entail not questioning my friendships with other guys. The second part would probably entail not showing up at my apartment. How about we start with those two things?"

That muscle in his jaw is working again and I wonder if he's going to explode from all that pent-up emotion. Finally, he looks me in the eye and his face relaxes, the corner of his mouth pulling up into a soft crooked smile.

"You haven't changed at all."

"Is that an insult?"

He shakes his head. "Quite the contrary."

I draw in a deep breath and let it out slowly as I stare at my helmet in my hands, unable to respond. When I look up again, I catch a glimpse of the inside of his forearm as he runs his fingers through his hair. He got the old tattoo partially covered. He quickly tucks his hand into his pocket so I can't make out the new tattoo.

"Let me give you a ride, Rory."

My stomach cramps at the idea of being alone with

him in the car again. "Does your wife know you're here?"

"Yes. I told her I had to give a friend a ride home."

"You lied to her?"

"About you being my friend?"

"About having to give me a ride home."

He smiles, his eyes lighting up with hope. "Does that mean we can be friends?"

"Houston... That hopeful look in your eyes is making me very uncomfortable."

He laughs and takes a step back. "Sorry. I guess I suck at this friendship thing. Maybe I can get some pointers from your friend... what was his name again?"

"I didn't tell you his name."

He bites his lip in a sheepish expression and my heart flutters with longing. I should *not* be alone with him. Ever.

He nods toward his car and smiles. "Come on."

I stare at his SUV for a moment and I suddenly remember the last time I gave him a blow job in his old Chevy truck. We were leaving a UO football game. The traffic around the stadium was horrendous and both our phones were dead, so I jokingly offered to strip for Houston to keep him entertained. He offered to do all the dinner dishes for a week if I followed through. Dishes being one of my least favorite chores, I quickly yanked up my green Oregon T-shirt and flashed my breasts at him.

"Houston, we have liftoff," he replied with a sexy grin.

I groaned as I tried not to laugh at his awful pun. Then I glanced around the crowded streets. When I was certain no one was looking in our direction, I ducked down to undo his jeans.

I chuckle to myself as I recall how crazy we were. "Thanks, but I have a ride," I say, tapping my handlebars. "See you later, Houston."

I pedal away, trying to pay attention to motorists while contemplating what just happened. Does Houston really want to be my friend? Does he only want to do what's best for his business? Or was he feeling me out to see if I'd be open to having an affair?

RACIÓN IS A Spanish tapas restaurant that's quite popular for its mastery of molecular gastronomy. I've never been to Ración, but I've read some of their reviews online and heard people talking about the place. The moment I walk in and see the tasting menu on the blackboard, I know this is going to be the kind of eatery that serves tiny portions that will break my budget.

I'm starving, since I normally have a late lunch when I get off work at four p.m., but I skipped lunch today to save my appetite for this special dinner. I love food, which is why I ride my bike to work most days, even when it's raining. So I can burn enough calories to justify my need to stuff my face.

I rode my bike to the restaurant tonight. I figure if I get a little tipsy, the worst-case scenario is I have to push my bike to the bus stop or the rail station. It will take me forty minutes to get home instead of fifteen. No big deal.

Kenny stands up and waves at me from the far left end of the bar. I make my way over, taking in the laid-back attire most people are wearing. A lot of vintage dresses paired with cardigans, plaid shirts and thrift-store jeans, and Gor-Tex jackets. I sigh with relief as I dressed pretty casually in my only pair of designer skinny jeans, an airy coral blouse, and some nude flats.

Kenny bumps his cheek to mine and wraps his arm around my shoulder. "Everyone, this is my gorgeous friend, Rory, short for Aurora." He stretches the syllables on my given name and I try not to blush. "Some of you may remember her from that one wonderful night in March when she graced us with her presence. Well, it only took five months for me to convince her to give us another shot."

I wave as everyone says hi, some of them offering me a handshake. Kenny asks Judy, the girl sitting next to him, to scoot over so I can sit next to him, then he orders me a Looking Glass cocktail.

"What's a Looking Glass?"

He shakes his head. "All you need to know is it contains absinthe. You'll like it."

Two drinks later, Judy and two of her dining companions have to leave and a group of three guys is seated at the bar on my right. The guy seated next to me has a full beard, which I've come to appreciate after two years living in Portland. Around here, growing a beard is a pissing contest; the fuller and longer the beard, the more virile and manly you are. It's cute to see men publicly fluffing their feathers in an attempt to attract mates.

The guy glances sideways and catches me staring at him. I quickly look away, but not before I catch a glimpse of his smile and the perfect teeth underneath that beard. I press my lips to keep from smiling and I hook my arm around Kenny, my social lifeline.

Kenny turns to me and smiles. "Are you having fun?" His eyes widen when I reply with a clumsy nod. "Oh, my goodness, Rory. Are you drunk off two cocktails?"

"Cocktails? Why do they call them *cock*-tails?"

"Oh, you're too adorable." He waves at a waiter, who quickly comes over. "Can you please hurry with the food?" He nods toward me and the waiter nods back, as if he can divine how tipsy I am with a single glance. "Thanks, man," Kenny calls out as the waiter walks away.

"Thanks," I mutter. "I'm starving."

"Then you came to the wrong place."

I whip my head to the right and Beard-guy is sporting a twinkle in his eye, looking very pleased with his comment as he takes a sip from his beer. I slip my left arm out of Kenny's and sit up straight so I can respond.

"Excuse me?"

He smiles, showing off those perfect teeth again. "I said you came to the wrong place if you're hungry. This place is for tasting, not eating."

"Are you saying I have to spit my food out after I taste it?"

He chuckles as he sets down his beer and turns his shoulders a bit so he can get a better look at me. His eyebrows scrunch up. "Rory?"

I squint at him through the dim lighting and I can just barely make out the crystal blueness of his eyes. "Do I know you?"

"You probably don't recognize me because of the beard." He holds his hands up to cover the lower half of his face.

My eyes widen with surprise. "Liam?"

He drops his hands and smiles. "In the flesh."

I lick my partially numb lips and reach for my glass of water, taking a few gulps before I set the glass down. "How long have you lived here?"

Liam was in my Art of the Sentence class junior year. We partnered up during an exercise where the professor asked us to construct a five-sentence-minimum short story. The catch was that it had to be done one word at a time, going back and forth for each word. The experience was memorable. Liam and I met at the local Starbucks and spent four hours sipping lattes and laughing at our ridiculous short story.

It was the first time I'd felt comfortable in the company of a man since Houston had left almost two years earlier. I was having such a good time, I didn't even notice he kept hitting the ignore button on his phone. Until we left Starbucks and he apologized before making a quick phone call—to his girlfriend.

"I actually just moved here a few months ago," he replies. "Got a job at Intel."

"Intel? What do you do there?"

He smiles as he reaches for his beer. "Corporate affairs. Totally boring. What are you doing these days? Still writing?"

Nothing like a question about what I'm doing with my career to sober me up. "I work at Zucker's for now. Yeah, I'm still writing."

"Zucker's? The grocery store on Burnside?"

"Actually, the one across the river on Belmont. But, yeah. It's temporary, you know, just until... I don't know. Until I decide it's not temporary, I guess."

He flashes me a reassuring smile. "Nothing wrong with that. I actually wish I had done something a bit more temporary. It's easy to feel trapped once you're in a so-called dream job. Competition is fierce. The pressure is on not to screw up."

I raise my eyebrows in agreement. "Yeah, I know that pressure."

"Are you...?" He looks down at my hands and smiles. "You're not married?"

I glance down and his left ring finger is bare, but his right hand is concealed behind the glass of beer he's holding. "No, are you?"

"Nope. I dodged that bullet shortly after graduation."

"Dodged that bullet?"

He laughs and takes another sip of beer as he tries to think of a response. "It ran its course."

I nod as if I understand what this means. The waiter arrives with our first course and I'm a little perplexed by what looks like a shallow bowl of purple goop.

Kenny gives my forearm a light squeeze. "Purple potato. Dig in, sweetheart. I can't have you passing out on me."

I turn to Liam and he looks confused as to why I was chatting him up if I'm here with someone. "This is my friend Kenny. We work together."

Kenny turns his head at the mention of his name, and his eyes twinkle as the sight of Liam. "Pleased to meet you," he says, reaching his hand out to Liam.

I lean back so they can shake hands and I get a weird feeling, like Kenny is sizing Liam up to see if he's good enough for me. And my suspicions are cleared up as soon as Kenny opens his mouth again.

"If you hurt her, I'll cut you."

"Kenny!" I squeal, but Liam just laughs as he goes back to nursing his beer. "He's kidding. He wouldn't hurt a fly."

"I've got your back, gorgeous," Kenny whispers in my ear, then he goes back to chatting with his friend George.

After a delicious, but slightly unsatisfying, five-course meal, Kenny insists on paying my $134 bill. He gives me a warm hug and I thank him profusely before I stand up to leave.

Liam grabs my hand as I begin to walk away. "Wait up. I'll give you a ride."

I glance at Kenny and his eyebrows are raised skeptically, then I turn back to Liam. "I rode my bike."

"I have a truck. We can put your bike in the back."

Liam quickly settles his bill and Kenny blows me a kiss as we head out.

"I'm really not that far," I insist as we head south on Washington.

"Yeah, but it's late. You shouldn't be riding alone at this time of night."

A desperate chill has fallen over the streets of Southwest Portland, fluttering the sleeves of my coral blouse. I rub my arms to warm up and Liam quickly removes his gray twill jacket.

"Put this on."

"I'm fine."

"Are you always this stubborn?"

"Yes."

He stops in the middle of the sidewalk and holds up the jacket for me. I roll my eyes as I slip my arms inside. But my reluctance quickly melts away as I'm comforted by the residual warmth and crisp scent left from his skin.

"See, that wasn't so bad, was it?"

"It's awful. I'll need therapy after this."

I unlock my bike and he pushes it for me toward his truck. Once he's satisfied that the bike is secure in the truck bed, we hop inside and head toward my apartment.

"Can I ask you a question?" he asks as we come to a stop at the first intersection.

I sigh as I anticipate a question about why I'm single or something else equally awkward. "Shoot."

"I never asked you this when we were partners in class, but I remember what happened to your friend freshman year. It was one of those things that people talk about for a week or so, then it gets forgotten. But I imagine it was quite different for you."

I clench my fist, digging my fingernails into my hand. "Is that a question?"

"Sorry. Actually, what I wanted to ask is… how are you doing?"

I'm silent for a moment as I contemplate his question. It's not an inappropriate thing to ask. It's actually a very intimate question, which I'm not obligated to answer. But he does seem genuinely concerned. And somehow, I find myself wanting to tell him the truth, that sometimes I still lie awake replaying the last few days I spent with Hallie over and over in my mind.

"Like you said, it's just one of those things," I reply, hoping he doesn't hear the painful thickness in my voice. "You learn to live with it."

Liam makes small talk the rest of the eight-minute ride to my apartment. Once we're in front of my building, he scoops the bike out of the truck bed and sets it down gently in front of me.

"Thanks for the ride." I begin to peel off his jacket and he holds up his hand to stop me.

"Keep it. I'll get it back next weekend, when you let me take you out."

I sigh audibly because I hate having to reject guys. "Liam, I'm not the kind of girl that can be saved. I'm beyond damaged… I'm destroyed."

"Damaged goods, huh?" he replies with a smile. "Does that mean I get a discount? Can I take you to McDonald's instead of Ración?"

I try not to smile. "I'm serious. I… I pretty much swore off relationships five years ago. I'm a lost cause."

He laughs at this. "Rory, you're twenty-four years old. We're all lost at this age." He reaches forward and my skin prickles as he brushes a lock of hair away from my temple and tucks it behind my ear. "Let me take you out and I'll decide whether you're defective."

As I gaze into his crystal-blue eyes, my mind drifts to thoughts of Houston. Earlier today, I refused to let him give me a ride home. But I allowed Liam to give me a ride. Does that mean I feel safer with Liam? And by safe, do I mean children's book safe?

I guess it doesn't matter what I mean. It just matters that he's the kind of guy my mom would want me to date. Maybe this will get her off my back.

"Okay."

His eyes light up. "Awesome. I'll pick you up here at eight next Saturday. Is that good?"

"Maybe... Maybe you should just come over and hang out. I haven't been on a date in a long time. I think I need to ease my way back into this."

He chuckles. "Well, you're definitely out of practice. Because, while I have no problem hanging out with you in your apartment, that's usually what happens *after* the date."

I shake my head in dismay at my own ignorance, but I don't offer to change the plans. I still think I'd feel more comfortable with him in my domain than surrounded by a bunch of strangers.

We quickly exchange phone numbers before I head inside. As I enter the elevator, a thought occurs to me that I hadn't considered before. If I'm dating other guys, that will make it much easier to resist Houston once we start working together.

Houston

Five years ago, April 5th

RORY WAS BORN with an affliction I like to call spontaneous hugging syndrome. Whenever someone does something really nice for her, she can't help but throw her arms around them in a wild embrace. This affliction is one of my favorite things about her. Often I find myself conspiring to do something nice just so I can trigger her hug reflex.

Today I'm using the excuse of our four-month anniversary. I ordered her a custom nightgown bearing an image of her head on Britney Spears's body and Justin Timberlake kissing her cheek. Rory is mildly obsessed with Justin Timberlake. I like to pretend it makes me jealous, but I actually find it pretty fucking adorable. I guess I'm also hoping this surprise will detract from the fact that it's the four-month-and-one-day anniversary of the day Hallie died.

I open the front door of the apartment and call out, "Honey, I'm home!" But there's no answer.

I head past the kitchen toward the bedroom, my mind immediately concocting the worst-case scenario. Reaching the bedroom door, I open it slowly and find Rory curled up on the bed with her laptop open next to her. The blanket clutched in her fist, her auburn hair tumbling over her face. I would let her continue sleeping, but I know she'll feel even more awful if she doesn't finish whatever homework she was working on before she fell asleep.

I set the package containing the nightgown on the foot of the bed, then I take a seat on the edge of the mattress next to Rory. "Baby, wake up." I give her shoulder a light squeeze and she lets out a soft groan. "Rory, are you okay?"

I reach forward to push the hair out of her face and she shoves my hand away. "Don't touch me."

"What's wrong?" I should probably be asking her, *What did I do this time?*

She sits up and her eyes find the package wrapped in silver paper, but she doesn't look pleased. "Celebrating something?"

I don't bother responding. I know this is a jab at my attempt to distract her from yesterday's anniversary.

Most of the time, Rory is too smart for her own good. She can spot my hidden motives before I act on them. Most of the time, but not always.

"I just wanted to give you something that might cheer you up. It's a cheesy gift. You can toss it out if you don't want it."

"Cheer me up?" She glares at me and I know today is going to be a bad day. "You want me to cheer up, Houston, then how about you let me have a night out with my friends! Oh, no, you can't do that because the only friend I ever had is dead." She slams her laptop shut and kicks the gift onto the floor as she slides off the bed. "With no *fucking* explanation."

My heart clenches with guilt, but I follow closely behind her as she heads for the bathroom. "It's okay to be angry."

"I'm not angry. I'm furious."

She opens the medicine cabinet and immediately reaches for a bottle of allergy medicine, the one she uses when she can't sleep.

"It's okay to be furious, too. Everyone deals with death differently."

She dumps eight pills out of the bottle into the palm of her hand, then she turns to me with a wicked smile. "Everyone deals with death differently? Like the way some people choose to not deal with it at all?"

I resist the urge to lash out at her. "You can't take that many, Rory."

She glances at the tiny pink pills in her hand. "Well, the six I took earlier didn't keep you from waking me up."

"Rory, this is not the way to handle this."

"Fuck you! Who are you to tell me how to handle it when all you do is ignore it? She killed herself, Houston. She killed herself and she didn't have the decency to tell anyone why." Her hands begin to tremble as the tears stream down her cheeks and the pills fall into the sink. "Sometimes I hate her."

"Don't say that."

She grips the edge of the sink tightly, her shoulders leaping with each chest-racking sob. "I do. I hate her."

"Don't you fucking say that."

"Why?" she mewls. "I just want to know why."

The words in Hallie's suicide note scroll through my mind like closing credits in a movie. I could end Rory's misery right now if I wanted to, and I do. I hate seeing her suffer like this. But my baby sister confided her darkest secret to me in that suicide note and I will never betray her.

"You don't hate her," I say, stepping forward to place my hand on the small of her back.

She smacks my arm. "Why can't you just let me feel the way I want to feel?"

"How would she feel if she heard you say that?"

She turns her head to face me, her mouth gaping wide with shock. "Are you serious? Hallie *can't* hear, because she's dead, Houston. She's fucking dead."

"Stop that."

"What are you gonna do? Are you gonna hit me?"

I clench my jaw to keep myself from calling her all the foul names racing through my mind. "Stop it, Rory."

She places her hands on my chest, probably to push me, but I grab her wrists to stop her.

"I said stop it. Stop acting like a fucking child."

She laughs as she tries to free her wrists from my grip. "Is that what I am to you? A fucking child? Is that why you love getting my underage ass drunk so you can fuck me?"

I glare at her for a moment, a million insults about her sexual inexperience teasing the tip of my tongue. Instead, I let go of her wrists and leave the bathroom.

"Where are you going?" she shouts as she follows me. "Going to get drunk and fuck another underage piece of ass?"

"Fuck you." I'm almost at the front door when she lands a hard shove in the center of my back. I round on her, grabbing both her elbows. "I told you to fucking stop it! That's enough!"

Her hazel eyes are wide with fright, but she's not ready to back down. "What are you gonna do?"

Our chests are heaving as we stare into each other's eyes and that's when I know there's no one in this world who will ever understand me like Rory. She knows I'd never hurt her. She knows she can rail against my sister and I'll still want nothing and no one but her. Because no one but me knows how brightly the pain burns inside her.

I let go of her elbows and tangle my fingers in her hair as I crush my lips against hers. I grab a fistful of hair at the crown of her head and tug. She whimpers as she reaches for the button of my jeans. Our mouths nip at each other clumsily as we frantically undress each other.

"I'm sorry," she whispers.

I shush her as I lift her naked body onto the kitchen table. Her legs coil around my hips and I hook my arm tightly around her waist as I slide into her. She moans and the sound sends a chill through me.

"God, I fuckin' love you."

She whimpers as I thrust my cock deeper inside her.

"I'm so sorry," she whispers a few more times, until I kiss her to silence her apologies.

She moans into my mouth and the sound is so damn beautiful it sends a shiver through me. I pull my head back and grasp her jaw in one hand so I can look her in the eye as I slide my other hand between her legs.

She gasps. "Oh, God, Houston."

I stroke her firmly as I move in and out of her until I feel her muscles spasming around my cock. I pull out of her and get down on one knee so my head is between her legs. Then I slide two fingers inside her as my mouth devours her swollen clit.

Her legs squirm and she screams my name with

ecstasy. When I slide into her again, I feel as if I might collapse from the pure euphoria of being inside her. She grabs my face and kisses me hard, but I can hear her cries have changed. I tilt my head back to look at her face and she's on the verge of sobbing. I sweep her hair away from her eyes and I move slowly in and out of her as I kiss each of her eyelids.

"It's okay," I assure her and her legs coil tighter around me, her arms squeezing me closer. "It's okay, baby."

"I love you," she whispers in my ear as I come inside her. "So much it scares me."

I kiss the tip of her nose, then lean my forehead against hers. "You don't have to be afraid… I'll never leave you."

Rory

Five years ago, April 6th

MY HEAD TWITCHES to the left, but it takes me a moment to realize what's happening. There's something on my face. I let out a piercing shriek as I try to bat away whatever spider or fly is perched on my eyebrow, then I freeze when I hear soft laughter.

I open my eyes and Houston breaks into a full cackle. "Was that you?"

"Sorry," he says, trying to keep a straight face. "I was just brushing your eyebrow with my finger to wake you up."

"You jerk. What time is it?"

"It's 6:30." He holds his arms out and beckons me to come closer. "Come here. You don't have to get ready for class for another hour."

I scoot in next to him and drape my arm across his solid chest. "Is it really 6:30?"

"Yep. Are you still tired?"

"I haven't slept that well in... months."

I trace my finger down the center of his chest, smiling as goose bumps sprout over his skin.

"I'm glad you slept," he says, kissing the top of my head.

"I'm sorry about the things I said yesterday," I whisper, my voice choked with regret. "I didn't mean it."

"No need to apologize," he murmurs. "Sometimes... Sometimes I get angry with her, too."

"She doesn't deserve that."

"No, she doesn't."

I trace a heart shape over his firm abs and smile when I see his erection rising beneath the sheet. I lightly rake my fingers over his ribs and back up to his chest. Then I trace the letters of the tattoo that stretches from one side of his chest to the other: LOYALTY. His other tattoo is on the inside of his left forearm: REMEMBER. Followed by the date Hallie died. He got both tattoos within the past six months.

Though he almost always avoids talking about Hallie, I know he hasn't forgotten her. And I know he's dealing with this in his own way. I shouldn't have accused him of avoiding the issue. But I do hope he'll open up to me at some point. I don't know if it's realistic to hope for something like that.

I take a deep breath and decide to give it a shot. "Remember that time Hallie got an iPod for Christmas?"

He lets out a soft puff of laughter. "Yeah, and she gave it to your grandma."

"I didn't even notice until the day after Christmas. My grandma was wearing headphones when I went to hug her goodbye."

"She was always way too mature for her age."

"My grandma?"

He laughs again, squeezing my shoulder as he plants a kiss on my forehead. "Remember when we used to go to the public pool and I had to discipline that fucking eight-year-old kid for staring at her?"

"She was thirteen and too pretty for her own good, but she loved the attention." I smile as I recall those summers I spent in Hallie's shadow. "I, on the other hand, hated the pool. All I wanted to do while I was there was watch you, but you never paid me any attention. No matter what bikini I wore."

"Maybe that was the problem. I would have noticed you if you weren't wearing a bikini."

I shake my head as I slide my hand under the sheet and wrap my fingers around his erection. A grin spreads across my face as I realize I finally got all I ever wished for during those summers at the pool. But the smile quickly disappears when I realize it was at the expense of my best friend's life.

I slide my fist down the length of his erection and his breathing quickens, but he reaches down and pulls my hand up.

He lifts my chin so I'm looking up at him. "I'm sorry."

"For what?"

"For never noticing you. If I had known… maybe everything would have turned out differently."

I snuggle up closer to him so I can whisper in his ear. "Different isn't always better."

BY THE TIME Houston pulls his truck into the lot of the sports bar, I'm ready to tell him to turn around and take me home, but I hold my tongue. It's been four nights since our blowout fight over Hallie and I've been trying to keep the peace. I kept my cool when he got drunk last night and asked me, in front of all his friends, if I wanted to fuck him in the bathroom. And I kept quiet when we slid into bed a couple of hours later and he accused me of flirting with his best friend, Troy. I'll just promise to give him a really long blow job if he agrees to be the designated driver tonight.

God, sometimes I hate the person I've become.

"What's tonight's forecast?" Houston asks as he kills

the engine.

"Rainy with a ninety percent chance of beer," Troy replies from the backseat.

"Just another night of grueling research," Houston replies and all I can do is roll my eyes.

As soon as we're seated at a table in the bar, I lay my hand on top of Houston's thigh and lean in to whisper my proposition in his ear. He grins broadly and Troy just shakes his head.

"Is that a yes?" I say, taking a sip from my glass of water.

He turns to me and his smile is gone. "If you don't want to watch me drink, you can take the truck home. I'll call a taxi."

He slides his car key across the table and bile rises in my throat as I stare at it. He's lost all perspective.

I know Houston took the brunt of the impact from Hallie's death. He was her older brother. He was supposed to protect her. He wasn't supposed to find her dead body in our dorm. He's probably suffering from post-traumatic stress disorder, but he refuses to see a therapist. He thinks this obsession with creating and consuming craft beer is a healthy alternative to therapy.

I don't know how much longer I can pretend everything's okay.

I take the key from the table and smile as I tuck it into my pocket. "I'll drive us both home... later."

"How about me?" Troy asks, leaning back in his

chair so he can check out the waitress serving beers at the table next to us.

Troy is Houston's oldest and best friend. They met in ninth grade around the same time Hallie and I met in sixth grade. Hallie had a crush on Troy for about two minutes when she was fourteen, before she decided he was too young for her. Hallie always had a thing for older men.

"Maybe you can get *her* to drive you home," I remark, and the waitress turns around.

Her glossy lips curl into a seductive smile as she catches Troy staring at her ass. Troy nods at her and she shakes her head as she walks off with her empty tray. His eyes are locked on her as she leans over the bar, flirting with the bartender while stealing the occasional glance in Troy's direction.

He stands up and pushes up the sleeves of his hoodie to expose his muscular arms. "I'll be back."

"You'd better come back with a pint," Houston calls out as Troy walks away.

He turns to me and the corner of his mouth turns up in that signature crooked smile. He leans forward and kisses my cheekbone. His lips hover over mine and suddenly I'm grinning like an idiot.

"You look beautiful tonight." He plants a tender kiss on my lips and I wish we were home so I could make out with him for hours. "I'll drive us home. You can be my beer taster and I'll be your designated driver."

He kisses me again and there's no way I can resist him when he's laying on the charm like this.

Another waitress arrives with the two pints we ordered earlier and Houston pushes the one she placed in front of him over to me. The waitress smiles and apologizes for mixing up the order.

"No worries," he says, waving off the apology. "My wife is planning on pounding about a dozen of these tonight, so keep 'em comin'."

I shove Houston and the waitress just smiles as she walks away. "Way to make me look like a lush."

"You're not even going to mention the fact that I called you my wife?"

I don't know how to respond to this. I didn't mention it because I assumed it was just part of the joke; it's funnier if you say *wife* than *girlfriend*. But now that he's calling attention to it, I don't know what to think.

I shrug as I lean in to take a sip of the farmhouse ale. "It was part of the joke."

He waits for me to swallow my ale, then he grabs my hand. "One day, we're going to get married. You know that, right?"

I chuckle and roll my eyes. "Yeah, of course."

"Did you just roll your eyes?"

"I just think it's a bit early to be making those kinds of proclamations. It's probably best not to make any promises we can't keep."

His gaze falls to the table and he nods. "You're

right." For a moment, I think this is it. The topic has been closed to further discussion. Then he sits up a little straighter and looks me in the eye. "No, you and I are going to be together forever. Even if we break up, we'll always make it back to each other; mark my words."

I nod as I reach for the beer again. "Do you want to know what I think of this beer?"

He smiles at my attempt to change the subject. "Shoot."

"It's too citrusy. You can taste a hint of honey, maybe even caramel, but the top notes are definitely orange and bitter lemon. The hops deliver a bite and they're lingering."

"IBU?" he asks.

IBU is an acronym for International Bittering Units, a measurement of the amount of bitterness or "hoppyness" in a beer.

"Probably thirty to forty."

He shakes his head. "I'm in love with a beer snob."

"Does that turn you on?"

"Put your hand under the table and you'll feel my beer-ection."

I almost spit out my ale, but I manage to swallow it down. Houston laughs as I grab the cocktail napkin to wipe the dribble from my chin. Then he rubs my back as I cough out the small bit of farmhouse ale I inhaled.

"That's what you get for killing Mufasa," he says.

I shake my head as I take another long sip of ale to

cool my throat, then an idea comes to me. "Did you decide what you're doing next week?"

"For Spring Break?"

"No, for Christmas," I reply sarcastically. "Of course for Spring Break."

He looks uncomfortable with this question. "Troy and I made plans."

"What kind of plans?" I regret the question as soon as it comes out. I don't want to be the nosy, clingy girlfriend. That's not me.

"Troy and I are gonna try out some new formulas."

"But... you guys do that every weekend."

The muscle in his jaw twitches and that's my signal to let it go. I want to say, *So that whole thing about us being together forever is only true if we never get too close?* but I hold my tongue... again. Then I down four more beers and give my detailed analysis of each one. Houston drives us home and fucks me over the bathroom sink. And when we wake the next morning, with the rain tapping on our bedroom window, Houston's head is lying on my abdomen, facing the foot of the bed.

I can't see his face so I reach down and run my fingers through his hair to wake him gently. At first, I think he's still sleeping. Then I hear a small sniff and I feel the wetness on my skin. This is the second time I've seen Houston cry and, somehow, this time is worse than the day Hallie died. Because today I don't know why, and I don't know if I ever will.

Houston

August 17th

LOVE IS A strange concept. That the very sight of someone, the very mention of their name, can cause an intense chemical reaction inside you is crazy. The fact that many people settle for less than that explosive chemical reaction is even crazier. Yet here I am, sitting next to Tessa in church on Sunday, praying to a god I stopped believing in five years ago.

Why am I sitting here watching people line up to eat a piece of bread impersonating the body of Christ? Because I'm afraid of what would happen if I weren't here. In other words, I'm afraid of becoming a cheating bastard like my father.

When I met Tessa at that beer festival three years

ago, I recognized something in her. Something we both shared: the need to forget. And I knew that, having honed that skill over the previous two years since Rory and I broke up, I had to be the one to teach Tessa how to do it.

I'll admit that the lessons were mutually beneficial in the beginning. But once Tessa began to put her brother's death behind her, I recognized something even more important in her: We had nothing in common other than our mutual grief, which we had so cleverly locked away.

I glance sideways at her and even the way she sits in the pew with her ankles crossed and her blonde hair hanging over her shoulders in perfect loose curls makes me bristle. I want to grab her slender shoulders and shake her and ask her why we're still pretending to love each other.

After we consume our piece of the Lord, we make it out to the parking lot before He's even dissolved on our tongues. We walk in silence as the warm summer breeze rustles the trees along the edge of the lot. I open the car door for Tessa and she raises one eyebrow.

"What's with the chivalry?"

I want to make a joke, maybe call her m'lady, but I can't muster up the energy to force the words out. "We need to talk."

She climbs into the car and stares straight ahead through the windshield. "Okay. Let's talk."

I shut the passenger door and hurry around to climb

into the driver's side. Once my door is closed, the sound of the breeze disappears and the silence takes a seat between us. I swallow hard as I try to think of how to start this conversation, but I'm dumbstruck.

Tessa knows nothing about Rory other than the few photos she's seen in Hallie's room of Rory and Hallie together. I asked my parents to destroy the few pictures they had of Rory and me. And I put all my own pictures of us on a flash drive I keep hidden in my office at the brewery. How do I even begin to explain to Tessa the kind of love I shared with Rory?

"Fine. If you're just going to sit there silent, then, yes. Yes, I contacted a fertility clinic. Are you really so mad you can't even speak?"

My vision blurs as my heart thumps inside my skull. "You... contacted a fertility clinic?" I turn toward her and she looks confused. "What the fuck were you thinking?"

"You... didn't know?"

"What were you thinking, Tessa? You went to a fucking fertility clinic without my consent?"

Her eyes widen with sheer terror. "I thought you knew. I thought that's what you wanted to talk about."

"You thought I knew? How the fuck was I supposed to know if you were *hiding* it from me?"

"But, I thought... I thought that's why you... you didn't come inside me. I... I thought you had looked at my laptop when I went to the appointment."

"You thought that's why I didn't come inside you? I didn't come inside you because I don't *want* to have a child. What is so fucking difficult to understand?"

"I thought you would change your mind! All young guys think they don't want children, but I've seen you with my nieces. You'd make a great father, Houston." She reaches for my hand and I yank it back before she can touch me. "Houston, please. Let's do this… together."

"Or what? Or you'll do it alone? When were you planning on telling me about going to the clinic? *After* you get pregnant?"

She turns away to look out the passenger window and a sick knot of fear grips my insides. "I'm four weeks along."

I'm tempted to tell her to get the fuck out of the car. Instead, I turn the key in the ignition and pull out of the lot without another word. By the time we get home, I know there's no way I can go inside with her. I leave her in front of the building, then I head for the brewery.

Twenty minutes later, I pull into a parking space in back of Barley Legal headquarters in Northwest Portland. On the outside, it looks like an old three-story shoebox brick building, which takes up half a city block in the industrial district. But on the inside, that's where all the magic happens.

I began brewing my own beer my sophomore year at UO. I majored in business with the idea of going to law school after graduation and subsequently selling my soul to the legal interests of corporations. But a girl I was dating that year gave me a dinky little home-brew starter kit. She knew my friends and I were beer snobs, so it was actually a pretty thoughtful gift. That relationship didn't survive past the new year, but I still have that starter kit in my office here at the brewery.

I enter through the back door and quickly punch in the code to shut off the alarm. No one comes in through the back on Sundays. Only the front and side entrances are open to let in the servers, management, and customers at the Barley Legal Brewhouse pub and restaurant. They won't even know I'm here.

I take the stairs up to the offices on the third floor. I pass the glass receptionist's desk, where Tessa worked for two weeks last year before she decided she preferred being a stay-at-home wife. I never had a problem with Tessa's choice to stay home. I make more than enough to support us. But I've always wondered how she can stand not having anything to do.

Tessa does have hobbies. She works out at the gym on the first floor of our building one to two hours a day with Kendra. Kendra's husband is a network security consultant who works from home, but they have a nanny who watches the baby while she's at the gym. Tessa also likes to make handmade event invitations. She takes orders on Etsy.com, where she gets an order once or twice a month. As I enter my corner office, I can't help but wonder if she'll be making her own baby shower invitations soon.

Just the thought of it makes my palms sweat. I can't have a baby with Tessa, but I also can't ask her to terminate the pregnancy. If Tessa's Catholic parents find out I "made" her get an abortion, I'll never hear the end of it.

I head for the corner of the office and open the closet door where I hang my coats and spare clothes and shoes. You never know when someone's going to spill some beer on you. And the Portland weather often leaves me craving a dry set of clothes. I reach into the back of the top shelf and feel around the dusty surface until I find the small tin box.

I take the box to my desk and set it down on the glass surface. Taking a seat, I lean back in my chair and stare at the box for a moment, as if gazing at it will tell me whether or not I should open it. I should call Troy and ask him to come have a beer with me. But I can't talk to him about Tessa tricking me into getting her pregnant. He'll say, *I told you so. Contessa Dracula sank her teeth in and now she's gonna suck you dry.*

Troy likes to call Tessa by her full name, Contessa. When she's not around he tacks on Dracula because he has insisted, from the day Tessa and I met, that she's after my money. She's not. Her parents do pretty well. Her dad's a pediatrician and her mom was a stay-at-home mom to their four children. Tessa is the youngest and therefore the most spoiled of them all. The oldest of the four, Jasen, is the one who died in a car accident four years ago.

But Troy and Tessa share a mutual dislike for each other. Troy has been my best friend since ninth grade, and he's always been a man-whore. He even gave me a run for my money after Rory and I broke up and I was fucking anything that moved. But he's actually been in a steady relationship for more than a year now, so you'd think Tessa would no longer feel the need to tense up every time I tell her I'm going out for beers with Troy. The problem is that he claims he's never going to get married. And he actually managed to find a smart girl who is willing to stay with him despite this.

Now, with Tessa pulling this baby crap on me, I'm wondering if women view these sorts of proclamations as temporary obstacles. Maybe Troy's girlfriend is only waiting until the right moment, until their lives are completely commingled, then she's going to spring the ultimatum: Marry me or get out of my life.

I grab the metal box off the desk and hold it up at eye level. Every picture I ever took of Rory is stored on a tiny flash drive inside this box. But I can't figure out if I should pop it into my laptop and let my mind wander back to the happiest and most miserable time of my life, or if I should toss it in the waste bin.

I'll never have the balls to leave Tessa if we have a child. I know this about me and she definitely knows this about me. So maybe I should just get it over with now. Completely erase Rory from my life and move on.

The lid on the box is embossed with a forest scene. In the center is a painted logo for Sierra Nevada Brewery. A chill passes through me as I slowly pry the lid off. I lift it away and set it down on the desk as I stare at the two objects in the box: a simple white USB flash drive and a three-carat princess-cut diamond engagement ring.

I had every reason to take this ring back to the jeweler after Rory and I broke up. I'd saved up almost every single penny of the money Troy and I made at our "beer tastings." We had a cover charge to get in, but once you were in, it was all-you-can-drink. We financed production of the home brew with our meager savings, so the money we made on cover charges seemed like pure profit.

After graduation, Troy used half his money to get a new car. Three weeks before graduation, I used about three-quarters of my earnings to buy this ring for Rory. I kept worrying about what would happen to us once I graduated and moved two hours away to start the brewery. I foolishly thought that an engagement ring would keep her committed to me while we were apart. But I didn't know how us staying together would work, logistically. I knew I could never go back to McMinnville with her. And I couldn't expect her to always visit her parents alone. So I kept the ring tucked away until I could figure it out.

Then a week later, she told me she was pregnant and I almost went through with it. I almost proposed. But I couldn't do it. Not to myself. Not to Hallie. And especially not to Rory.

"Hey, man. What are you doing?"

The sound of Troy's voice startles me and I drop the box into my lap. The ring and the flash drive tumble out and onto the wood floor. Troy's eyes immediately lock on the ring and I quickly get on my knees to retrieve it from beneath the desk.

"What's that? Renewing your vows with Contessa already?"

I bump my head on the glass as I get up. "*Fuck*. No, this is nothing. It's old." I drop the ring into the box and hastily put the lid back on. "What are you doing here?"

He has one eyebrow raised as he fixes me with a *stop-bullshitting-me* stare.

I sigh as I set the box on my lap to semi-hide it from Troy. "It's a ring I got for Rory... a long time ago."

"And you still have it?" he says, taking a seat in a chair on the other side of the desk.

I think of lying to him and saying the jeweler wouldn't let me return it, but that's such a load of crap. I don't think a kindergartner would believe that.

"I ran into her," I say as casually as I can.

"Who, Rory?"

I nod and he lets out a soft chuckle.

"Wow. Is she living in Portland?" he asks, his eyebrows perking up with curiosity.

I nod again as I place the metal box back on the desk. "I'm gonna be working with her."

"What the fuck? Did you *hire* her?"

"No! No, it's nothing like that. It's that wine bar."

"The contract we signed on Friday?"

"Yeah, she works at the market."

"Well, I'll be." Troy lets out a cackle of laughter as he smacks his knee. "There you fuckin' go, man. That's your ticket out. Now you can kick Contessa to the curb and get back with Rory."

"What the fuck are you talking about? I'm not going to divorce my wife because I ran into my ex-girlfriend."

"Then why the fuck are you sitting alone in your office staring at a ring you bought five years ago? Because if you're not planning on doing something with that ring, then that just seems pathetic."

I shake my head. "One of these days I'm gonna build a balcony just so I can throw you off."

"Yeah, yeah. Don't get mad at me. You're the one sitting here pining for a girl you could probably still have in a heartbeat. Unless she's with someone else. Is that what it is?"

"I don't know."

"Then find out." He stands from the chair and heads for the door. "I don't know much about relationships, but I know I've never seen you as miserable as you were when you two broke up. And I know I've never seen you as happy with Tessa as you were with Rory."

"Now you're calling her Tessa?"

"I'm trying to be serious. But whatever, dude. Do what you gotta do. I just came in to get my racket. Meeting Joey at the gym. Wanna come?"

"Nah, I'm good. I'm just gonna sit here and stare pathetically at this ring a bit longer."

He shrugs. "The lube is in my top drawer. Don't use it all."

"You take it. You'll need it when Joey makes you his bitch."

Troy walks away cackling and I lean forward to stare into the shallow depths of the tin box. He's right. Staring at this ring is pathetic.

But I can't keep it. It doesn't belong to me.

It's time to give it to its rightful owner.

Tessa

August 18th

KENDRA'S APARTMENT IS exactly the same as ours. The same two bedrooms with windows; her windows face the courtyard while ours face Savier Street. The same concrete counters and black kitchen cabinets. The same layout and, oddly enough, it even smells the same since she gifted me the same scented oil diffuser she uses. The one major difference is that her apartment is overrun with baby gear.

You walk in the door and, if you're not paying attention, you'll bump into the black stroller with the lime-green polka-dots. Her kitchen sink is always piled high with baby-food containers that she sterilized and set out to dry. I've never understood how they're supposed to remain sterile while drying in that dish rack. Her living room is cramped by a playpen and, half the time, her coffee table is pushed against the wall under the window so eight-month-old Trucker can crawl around without knocking his head on the furniture.

I take a seat on Kendra's overstuffed sofa and try not to stare at Trucker in his high chair. He has Kendra's dark hair and gray eyes, but his face is round and bright, just like Kendra's husband, Aaron. Aaron is a great guy, but he can be a bit abrasive sometimes, like Kendra. The few times Kendra has tried to get him to hang out with Houston and me, he accused her of trying to set him up on an adult playdate. Kendra gave up trying to force us into a four-way friendship months ago.

"So, I had to go to Aaron's cousin's house in Salem for a birthday party this weekend. So trashy. I swear, it's like I married the only sane person in that whole family. How was your weekend?" Kendra asks as she shovels a spoonful of organic pureed peas into Trucker's pursed baby lips.

I tear my eyes away from Trucker and sigh. "I told Houston I'm pregnant."

"You're pregnant? *Already?*"

"No, I lied to him."

"You what? Why?"

I get an itch on my forearm, but I know it's just the guilt irritating my scars, so I resist the urge to scratch. "Because I'm stupid. I thought he had found out about the appointment with the fertility clinic."

"Because he came home early?"

"Yeah. I was convinced he had opened up my laptop and saw the website in my history. Especially because, just a few days later, we were having sex and he pulled out for the first time since I had this IUD implanted fourteen months ago."

Kendra uses Trucker's bib to wipe away some green goop from the corner of his mouth, then she turns to me with a very suspicious look in her eyes. "He pulled out?"

"Yeah, I know. It freaked me out. But he was acting like it was no big deal, so I accused him of cheating on me."

"Oh, because that's always smart."

I lean forward and grab a travel magazine off the coffee table, which is right where it's supposed to be today. "I know. I've been doing a lot of stupid things ever since I had that consultation. Dr. Menlo told me that even if I take the IUD out now, I probably won't get pregnant for four to six months. And that's only if we track my ovulation patterns and have sex during peak times. I can't even get Houston to come inside me with an IUD. How am I ever supposed to have a baby?" I sigh heavily. "Why doesn't he want to have a baby with me?"

"He doesn't want to have a baby with anyone. You know that."

Kendra is referring to the conversation I had with

Ava Cavanaugh, Houston's mother, shortly before Houston and I got married two years and three months ago. Houston doesn't know his mother told me about the ex-girlfriend he got pregnant. According to Ava, they broke up right after the girl got an abortion. She wouldn't tell me the girl's name, but I got the feeling Ava loved her very much, which makes me even more insecure. The reason she divulged this information to me was as a cautionary tale. In other words, she was silently warning me, *If Houston didn't want children with her, then he will definitely never want children with you.*

I flip the travel magazine open to a random page and land on an advertisement for vacation rentals in Bali. "I know, but that's what all guys think."

"No, it's not, Tessa. Aaron and Houston are not all guys. Besides, once Aaron found out I was pregnant, he completely flipped sides and couldn't get enough of my juicy birth canal."

"Ew."

"Whatever. The point is that you have to accept that Houston doesn't want kids. And you have to emotionally prepare for the possibility that he may leave you if you do get pregnant without his consent or if he finds out you're bluffing about this pregnancy."

I turn another page and roll my eyes at the happy couple pictured next to an article about chic honeymoon locations. "You're the one who told me to get pregnant. Now you're telling me to consider the consequences?"

"I didn't tell you to get pregnant. All I said is that it worked for me. Results may vary. But I guess it doesn't matter what I think 'cause Houston is the type of guy who needs to be trapped or someone else is gonna sneak in there. He's totally Vanessa's type: hot, rich, and married. Like, you should totally keep him away from Vanessa or she'd be all like, 'Lawd! I'd let him ram me so hard my lunch would fall out.'"

My stomach curdles at the thought of Vanessa and Houston together. "Ugh. I hate that girl."

Vanessa is Aaron's sister, who likes to come over and visit Kendra every once in a while. She has a disgusting habit of dating married men. She claims it's because she likes excitement and expensive gifts, especially when they come without commitment. I think it's because she's a dirty home-wrecker.

Kendra pulls Trucker out of the high chair and he flashes her a gracious smile as she balances him on her hip. His gray eyes find me across the room and I smile, though I know his eyes aren't developed enough to see me clearly. His chubby hand smacks his mom's chest as she clears the bowl of food from the chair.

"Settle down, Trucker."

I set the magazine on the coffee table as I rise from the sofa. "I'll take him so you can clean up."

Kendra's brow furrows with pity as I hold my hands out to her and I know what she's thinking. And she's right.

She hands him over and I get a weird sensation in my chest the moment his soft body is snuggled against my hip and inside the crook of my arm. Trucker reaches for my hair and I gently grab his hand to redirect his attention. He smells so soft and clean with just a hint of sweet earthiness on his breath from the baby food. He nods at me and I nod back. Kendra has been teaching him to nod and shake his head as well as a few simple phrases in sign language. I don't know why Trucker's nodding at me, but I'd like to think it's because he approves of my prospects as a baby handler.

I just wish I could get Houston to feel the same.

Rory

My JAW DROPS when Jamie finishes making her offer. She waits patiently for me to respond, but after a couple of minutes of stunned silence, she finally has to speak.

"Is that a yes?"

"I… I can't run a wine bar."

"Yes, you can. If Theo can run the coffee bar, you can take over at the wine bar."

When Jamie pulled me into her office ten minutes ago, I never imagined she'd be offering me a management position. But that's exactly what she's done. Assistant manager of the wine bar at the Goose Hollow location. A seven-minute walk from my apartment. And more than twice what I'm currently making.

The current assistant manager of the coffee bar, Theo, is only nineteen years old and won't be allowed to keep the same position when it's converted into a wine bar. He's being promoted to Assistant Manager II of customer service. They need someone to take his place and, somehow, Jamie got it in her head that I would be perfect for this position.

"Why me? Isn't there anyone else at the Goose Hollow store you can promote?"

"So you don't want the promotion?"

My throat goes dry as I realize I'm botching this up. "No, I didn't say that. I was just wondering why… I… Oh, forget it. Yes, of course I want it. Thank you so much, Jamie. This is… amazing. Thank you."

She smiles and her crooked tooth shines under the fluorescent lighting in her office. "You're welcome. I'm sure you'll do great."

She winks at me as I get up to leave and I hold in my laughter as I exit her office. Then it hits me. What if that wink was meant in a wink-wink nudge-nudge sort of way? What if she was trying to tell me something? *Oh, God.* What if Houston is the one who told her to give me the management position?

No, that's crazy. As far as Jamie is concerned, Houston is just a supplier. He has no power over hiring decisions. And I'm flattering myself to think he would care enough to do something like recommending me for a management position. Besides, if he did recommend me for that promotion it was probably because he's planning on spending less time at the Goose Hollow location. Not the other way around.

I finish out my last day as a cashier at 4:37 p.m. when Kenny arrives to start his shift. I run into him in the warehouse as he's clocking in.

"Hey, sexy. You look happy. Did you finally get some?"

My happiness is quickly deflated when it dawns on me that I'm no longer going to see Kenny four to five times a week. "I got a promotion."

"To what?"

"Assistant manager of the wine bar…"

Kenny's gorgeous green eyes widen.

I continue, "In Goose Hollow. Today's my last day here."

"*WHAT?*"

"I know. I'm so sad I'm not going to see you anymore."

"What are you talking about? You're not getting rid of me that easily. But what in the fuckity-fuck is up with that promotion? I mean, don't get me wrong, it's not that you're not qualified. You're obviously *over*qualified for every position here." He winks at me, then continues. "But isn't a promotion like that a bit out of left field? Did you apply for the position or something?"

I shake my head. "No, I didn't know about any of this until Jamie called me into her office this morning."

Kenny shrugs and gives me a quick hug. "Doesn't matter. You deserve it. And now I have an excuse to stalk you—I mean *visit* you at your apartment."

"I'd love for you to visit me." A sudden urge overcomes me and I throw my arms around him again. He chuckles and I let go quickly.

"You're so weird, Rory."

"In a good way?"

"In a beautiful way. I'll call you later. You still have to tell me all about the lumberjack you went home with Sunday night."

A chill passes through me at the mention of Liam. He called me last night as I was getting into the shower, but I didn't call him back when I got out. I listened to his voicemail once before I deleted it, then I stared at my phone for about two hours while thinking of Houston.

My mind constantly draws back to the memory of him telling me that we would be together forever, even if we broke up. I held on to that memory like a totem of our relationship. An intangible relic. A wispy promise, easily forgotten and even more easily broken.

But we did make it back to each other, just like he said we would. Only now it's impossible for us to be together. Yet, he seems intent on having a presence in my life as some sort of heroic chauffeur. I laugh out loud at this thought and only then do I realize I'm still standing next to Kenny in the warehouse.

He shakes his head at me. "You need to get laid,

sweetheart."

I let out a deep sigh. "Working on it."

EVERY TIME THE phone rings I become more nervous. Until I'm so nervous I feel physically sick to my stomach. Finally, on the fourth ring, Liam answers.

"Rory?"

I suck in a sharp breath and my reply comes out far too high-pitched. "Liam! Hi!"

He chuckles. "Hi. How are you doing?"

Skippy yelps to tell me I'm scratching his head a bit too hard. "I'm fine. Just lying in bed with my dog. Wait. That sounded weird. I'm just relaxing. Yeah, that sounds better."

"Actually, I liked the visual of you lying in bed."

I swallow hard as I try to think of a response, but Liam laughs it off.

"Well, I could try to make some more small talk," he says, and I sense another proposition coming, "or you can invite me over."

"This whole dating thing is still kind of weird for me, so I'll need you to be patient."

"I don't do patient," he replies, and an awkward silence settles in between us, then he laughs. "I'm kidding. I've actually been sitting by my phone waiting for you to call me since I dropped you off last Sunday."

"Who sits by their phone anymore? Doesn't your phone sit by *you*?"

"I guess you're right. I'll have to work on the accuracy of my guilt-trip material. So how was your day?"

I sigh audibly. "Ugh. This sucks. I hate small talk."

"When I come over, I promise I'll only talk big."

"Talk big? What does that mean? Are you going to make bold claims about yourself all night?"

"If that's what you're into. I might even back up those claims with some action."

My face flushes with heat. "Don't get any funny ideas, okay? I barely know you and, like I said, I'm not looking for anything serious right now."

"That's fine with me. We can keep our relationship strictly based on shallow sexual encounters."

"Hanging up now."

I stare at the phone for a second wondering if this is a good idea. I haven't had sex with anyone since Houston. I know it's totally lame, but he was my first. And he was so patient with me that I quickly opened up to him. Less than a month into our relationship, we were trying things some couples would consider kinky. But I always felt safe and adored when I was with Houston. The idea of having sex with someone and not feeling that way doesn't appeal to me. I want to feel that intense emotional bond as well as the primal sexual attraction.

It's way too early to expect to feel that with Liam, so I'll have to ask him to take it slow. As I told him before, I'm damaged goods. I sigh heavily at this thought. Five years later and the pain is still as intense as it was the day Houston hand-fed me a bowl of soup then snuck out of our apartment in the middle of the night, when he thought I was sleeping.

I consider getting dolled up to hang out with Liam, but if he's going to like the real me, then a messy ponytail is the least disturbing part of me he's going to have to accept. As a small courtesy, I apply some powder and blush to my cheeks and some tinted lip balm. Skippy and I get settled down on the sofa with Animal Planet on the TV, but we're quickly interrupted by a knock at the door.

Skippy lets out a soft bark as he jumps down from the sofa.

I point at the cushion he just vacated. "Sit, Skippy."

He casts a forlorn glance in my direction before he hops back onto the sofa.

"Stay," I say, for good measure.

My heart is beating so fast and hard, I can feel my pulse in my fingertips. I reach for the knob and take a slow breath as I open the door.

My jaw drops. "Houston. What the hell are you doing here?"

I peek my head into the corridor and I'm only slightly relieved to see Liam hasn't arrived yet. But he'll be here any moment. I have to get Houston out of here.

"Were you expecting someone else?" He looks me up and down for a second, taking in my messy ponytail, gray leggings, and UO hoodie. "You look—"

He stops himself before he can finish this sentence and I find myself wondering if he was going to tell me I look pretty or that I look like shit. I want to ask him, but I don't have time.

"Houston, you need to leave."

"Are you expecting someone?" he replies, glancing toward the elevator.

"That's none of your business."

His jaw clenches. "I came to bring you something."

"Bring me something? Bring me *what*?"

His whole body seems to tense and that's when I notice his hands are clasped behind his back. Is he hiding something back there?

"What is it?" I whisper.

He gazes into my eyes for a moment and I'm flooded with a gust of raw emotion. I desperately want whatever he's going to give me.

"Houston, what is it?"

He opens his mouth to speak, but he's interrupted by the ding of the elevator. I whip my head to the right and I watch anxiously as Liam glances at the sign on the wall pointing him in our direction. He turns left and his eyes lock on Houston and me, then he proceeds toward us cautiously.

I don't know what to do. How do I introduce them to each other? *Liam, this is the ex-boyfriend who destroyed me. Houston, this is my new friend Liam, who I hope will help me get over you.*

Houston's hand closes around my elbow, but surprisingly I don't flinch. "Rory, you're trembling. Are you okay?"

Liam arrives and seems a bit confused, so I quickly push Houston's hand away. And now I'm shaking again, even more than I was before.

"I'm fine. Houston, this is my friend Liam." I turn to Liam and hope he can see the plea in my eyes to cut me some slack for this very awkward, unplanned encounter. "Liam, this is… my old friend Houston."

Houston narrows his eyes at my description of him, but after an awkward few seconds, he turns to Liam and offers him his hand. "Good to meet you."

Liam nods at him as they continue to shake hands. "You too."

Houston doesn't seem to be ready to let go of Liam's hand, so I finally grab Liam by the arm and pull him inside. His body is almost flush against mine, so close I can feel his warmth and smell his crisp scent. I whisper for him to go ahead and take a seat on the sofa and he smiles as he heads inside.

I shut the door behind me so I'm alone in the corridor with Houston. "I told you not to come here."

"Is that your boyfriend?"

"No, it's not my boyfriend. Actually, it's none of your business. You need to leave."

I reach for the doorknob and he grabs my hand to stop me. "Tell him to leave."

"Are you kidding me? No way."

"Do you see that?" He nods toward where his hand is covering mine. "You're not trembling anymore."

I slide my hand out from under his and shake my head. "No, Houston. You're married. You're not allowed to come here and fuck with my life. Go home."

He pulls his other hand out from behind his back and brandishes a small metal box with a Sierra Nevada logo on the top. He stares at the box for a moment before he holds it out to me.

I take the box from his hand and my heart sputters. There's something small and hard sliding around inside the box.

"What is it?"

"It's my promise to make this right." He takes a step toward me and I'm frozen as his hand lands on my cheek. He brushes his thumb softly over my cheekbone, then he leans in and plants a soft kiss on my forehead. "You look beautiful tonight."

I want to hurry inside the apartment so I don't have to watch him walking away, but I can't tear my gaze away from him. As I watch him getting into the elevator, I get the urge to run after him and kiss him. Instead, I close my eyes and listen to the soft swoosh of the elevator doors closing.

I heave a deep sigh as I turn around and head back inside the apartment. The sight of Liam sitting on my sofa with Skippy's head in his lap instantly puts me at ease.

"Is everything all right?" he asks, and I sense another question in there. *Do you want me to leave?*

I smile as I set the small metal box on top of the breakfast bar, then make my way to the sofa. "Never better."

I consider not asking Skippy to move, but that would mean I'd have to sit on the opposite end of the sofa from Liam. And right now I think I need to be close to someone. I gently order Skippy to get down and he begrudgingly obliges, then I take a seat on the middle cushion next to Liam.

"Do you like Animal Planet?" I ask, trying to keep my voice casual.

"I thought you asked me over here because you hate small talk." He smiles at me and I'm treated to the sight of his gorgeous teeth framed by his perfectly groomed beard.

"You want to know who that was?"

He shrugs and I take that as a yes.

I let out a soft sigh and continue. "He's the one... the one who changed everything."

"Oh." He nods as if he totally understands, but I can tell this information has made him uncomfortable. "So...

he wants to get back together?"

I glance at the metal box on the breakfast bar. "He wants to make things right, whatever that means."

"Is that possible—to make things right?"

I stare at Liam for a moment as I contemplate this question. "I don't know."

He smiles and I take the opportunity to scoot a bit closer to him. He quickly takes the hint and wraps his arm around me so I can lay my head on his shoulder. It's only ten p.m., but I can already feel myself getting very relaxed and sleepy in his arms. He must feel it too, because a few minutes later he kisses my forehead and uncoils his arm from around my shoulders.

"I should let you get to sleep."

"But you didn't get to talk big."

He chuckles as he stands from the sofa. I move to get up, but he holds his hand out to stop me. "Thanks for being honest with me, Rory."

"Why would I not be honest with you?"

He shakes his head. "You know, the thing about honest people is that they can't imagine why someone else would be dishonest."

"Are you calling me naive?"

He laughs again. "No. No way. I'm just saying that you're an honest person and… I find that very sexy."

"Sexy?"

He smiles, then heads for the door, leaving me feeling a bit unsatisfied with his twenty-minute visit.

Though, I get the feeling he's leaving out of a need for self-preservation. What did I expect? I invited him over and he found me talking to my ex-boyfriend in the doorway. Then I went and told him the truth, that I don't know if things can ever be made right between Houston and me. I should have lied and told him that Houston and I are irreparable.

Maybe Houston was right. Maybe we *will* always make it back together.

Then we'll never stop hurting each other.

Houston

August 23rd

I SIT IN my car for about five minutes, contemplating my next move. I consider waiting for Liam to leave. Maybe—hopefully—my presence scared him and he'll leave early. Then I consider going up there and dragging him outside where he can't touch her. But I lost my right to be territorial with Rory five years ago. Ultimately, I decide to take Rory's stern advice and go home to face my wife.

I pull out of the curved driveway in front of Rory's building and set off in the opposite direction of my apartment. I need to figure out how to approach Tessa before I get there. If there's one thing I've learned in two years of marriage, it's that you must have a plan when arguing with a woman. If you go in blind, you'll be knocked over the head and slaughtered before you know what hit you.

My mind draws back to the day I asked Tessa to marry me. We had been together a whopping four months before I decided that she was exactly the type of woman I needed to spend the rest of my life with. Someone who would stay with me no matter how often she suspected she should leave. Someone who wouldn't question why I was never fully hers.

It was December 4th, the third anniversary of Hallie's death. As always, my plans were to get so drunk that I blacked out. Tessa knew my sister had committed suicide, but she didn't know all the grisly details of how I found her. Or how the next six months I spent with Rory were the best and worst months of my existence. And she certainly didn't know about my tradition of getting blackout drunk on the anniversary of Hallie's death. So when Tessa tried calling and texting me a dozen times with no reply, she didn't know why I wasn't calling her back. And when she showed up at my apartment and found me shit-faced drunk, fucking a girl I'd met at a bar and took home because she reminded me of Rory, what she did next changed everything.

I expected Tessa to hit me, or the girl whose pussy was wrapped around my dick. I expected her to cry or storm out of my apartment. I expected her to do pretty much anything other than what she actually did.

She threatened to kill herself.

She told me, rather calmly, that if I didn't make the girl leave she would take her own life. She insisted that after losing her brother she wouldn't have anything to live for if she lost me, too. That was when I knew I couldn't leave her, and that I didn't really want to, because she didn't care if I loved her. She didn't care that I was still in love with Rory. All Tessa wanted was for me to stay with her. To me, this made her perfect.

It was quite a dramatic scene, getting the Rory lookalike out of the apartment and convincing Tessa that I was going to stay with her and she didn't need to kill herself. Dare I say I even relished the moment? It was a second chance to save her the way I couldn't save Hallie. Once Tessa was wrapped safely and calmly in my arms, I asked her to marry me right there. And she accepted, with no ring.

I had never felt more disgusted with myself and more relieved at the same time. The burden of trying to find someone to measure up to Rory was lifted. I could settle for someone who accepted me at my worst, as long as my worst was merely that I loved someone else from afar.

But showing up at Rory's apartment and presenting her with an engagement ring that's far more expensive than the ring I ultimately gave my wife is not quite "loving her from afar." And normally I would deal with this type of problem by drinking myself into unconsciousness, but all I can think of right now is *What would Rory want me to do?* She tolerated my drinking binges when we first got together, often trying to outdrink me. But by the end of our six-month relationship, just the sight of beer annoyed her.

Half of me wants to get blasted so I can deal with Tessa. Because I know she won't care. She'll probably use my drunken state to her advantage to try to have sex with me. The other half of me wants to stay sober so she knows I mean it when I tell her I'm leaving.

I'm leaving? This thought surprises me even though it originated in my mind. Am I really going to leave Tessa for getting pregnant behind my back? That would make me the worst husband in the history of Tessa's Catholic family. Maybe the more important question is: Am I going to leave Tessa because she deceived me into getting her pregnant or am I leaving her for Rory, and if I leave her… what will she do?

I get my answer as I'm pulling the SUV into the underground parking garage. A text message from Rory.

Rory: *This box won't stop staring at me.*

I smile for a split second as I imagine going back to Rory's and slipping the ring on her finger. Then I remember what happened the last time Tessa caught me cheating on her and my smile evaporates. I stare at the message for at least a minute before I respond.

Me: What's in the box?!

I hit send, hoping she'll understand the reference to Brad Pitt's famous line from the movie *Seven*. I always used that line whenever Rory ordered something online and the package arrived on our doorstep.

Rory: *If this box contains Gwyneth Paltrow's severed head I'm going to be very disappointed.*

I shake my head and grin like an idiot. She's still the same Rory I knew five years ago. I have to stop myself from responding with a dirty text about giving good head, the way I would have responded when we were together. Then I try to come up with a clever response, but after a couple of minutes I decide to call her instead. I'm surprised when she answers.

"Houston." The way she says my name, preceded by a small, reluctant sigh, makes me smile.

"Rory."

"What's in the box?"

This is the moment of truth. Whatever I say right now will change my marriage forever.

I draw in a long breath and she waits patiently as I let it out slowly. "I'd rather open it for you and show it to you myself."

She's silent for a moment. An excruciatingly long

moment. "Fine. I won't open it until tomorrow."

"Tomorrow?"

"That's when I start my new job. Are you saying you had nothing to do with me getting a promotion?"

I can't sneak anything past her.

"I may have had a little something to do with that. Are you upset?"

"Upset? Why would I be upset? Because I'm making double what I used to make and I can walk to work now? Yeah, I'm totally upset. I'm writing my manifesto right now before I go blow up the grocery store."

I smile though there's an ache inside me when I think of how much I've missed her quick comebacks.

"I knew I should have told Jamie to fire you instead. Is there anything I can do to make it right? Maybe I can help with that manifesto."

She's silent for a moment and I wonder if I've said something wrong. Then it dawns on me that she mentioned she was working on a book in her spare time.

"Rory?"

"Yeah?"

"What's your book about?"

She's silent again, but this time there's no fidgeting or background noise. As if my question has created a vacuum of space between us, sucking out all the sound and energy.

I glance at my phone to make sure the call didn't drop, then I bring it back to my ear. "Rory?"

"Yeah, I'm still here."

"You don't have to tell me. I was just being nosy."

"No, it's fine. I'll tell you what my book is about when you show me what's inside the box."

And just like that, all my trepidation over whether I should give Rory that ring disappears. Because I want to know what she's writing. I desperately want to know what's important enough for her to spend months or even years thinking about.

Who the fuck am I kidding? I want to know if she's writing about me. And, yes, I'd give up my marriage to find that out.

Rory

Five years ago, February 13th

THIS IS MY fifth trip to Barnes & Noble this week and I've come away empty-handed each time. I'm in a rut. I haven't read anything for two weeks straight. If I don't find something to keep my mind occupied outside of studying, I'll go crazy.

I trace my finger along the edge of the wooden table as I enter the Barnes & Noble off campus. The table is stacked with all the latest new releases from authors like Danielle Steel and J. D. Robb. Some nonfiction bestsellers are mixed in, but nothing that catches my eye.

Normally, I'd just pick up the latest book from one of my favorite authors, but I've read all the most current releases. And I'm not in the mood for the same type of romance or family drama I normally read. I'm trying to avoid that kind of story right now, seeing as I'm unable to escape those things in real life.

Tomorrow is my first Valentine's Day with Houston and he hasn't mentioned it at all. I've been silently obsessing over it for a few weeks now. Which is probably why I haven't been able to read for pleasure lately.

A hardcover near the back of the table grabs my attention and I pick it up to get a better look. The jacket cover depicts a quaint arched bridge set in front of a rich midnight-blue sky. A gray satin ribbon appears to be gently falling from the sky toward the glistening water under the bridge. I brush my thumb across the embossed title: *The Fall* by Amanda Cabot. I've never heard of this author, but I make an impulsive decision to buy the book without reading the description on the inside flap.

I pull up in front of our apartment building twenty minutes later and I'm surprised to see that Houston is parked next to the curb. We switch between parking at the curb and using the carport that came with the apartment. There's only space for one car in the carport, so he parks his truck in the space Friday through Sunday and I park my seven-year-old Toyota there Monday through Thursday. It's Friday evening, so he should be parked in the space tonight. I assume he's invited a friend over and they took the carport, so I park my car next to the curb behind Houston's truck and head inside.

I open the front door and I'm surprised to find Houston lying shirtless on the sofa with no one else around. "Are you alone?" I ask, throwing my keys and my backpack onto the kitchen table. I take my Barnes & Noble bag to the sofa and he sits up to make room for me.

"No, my imaginary girlfriend is in the shower."

"Why are you parked at the curb?"

He watches intently as I pull my new book out of the bag. "I forgot to park in the space and by the time I remembered I was already lying here in my boxers. I'll move it in the morning. What'd you get?"

"I don't know. I just picked a random book off the display table and bought it."

He laughs as he takes the book from my hand. "You're such a dork." He holds up the book and reads the title aloud. "*The Fall?* Sounds literary."

"I guess I'll find out soon. I'm gonna go take a bath."

I reach for the book and he holds it above his head so it's out of my reach. "What are you talking about? You can't read it without me. That's not fair."

I can't stop the stupid grin spreading across my cheeks. "Fine. But I have to take a shower. I smell like the smoker dude who sat in front of me in the lecture hall today."

He narrows his eyes at me. "What were you *doing* with the smoker dude?"

"Oh, you know, the usual bj followed by lots of cuddling."

I stand up to go to the bathroom and Houston grabs my hand. "I'll cuddle with you, Scar."

"But will you give me a bj?"

He lets go of my hand and smacks my ass. "Go take a shower, dirty girl. I'll get the bed ready for your bj."

Houston

Five years ago, February 13th

WHENEVER RORY STARTS reading a new book, she always wants to read the story aloud to me. I think it's cute, but I've never cared for women's fiction or romance, which is what she mostly reads. A month ago, after shooting down her fourth request to read to me, I told her I'd only listen if she took off all her clothes while she read. I thought she'd get a little pissed, then resume her book without me. I didn't expect her to say yes.

I've acquired a new appreciation for women's fiction and romance ever since then. Especially the love scenes. No matter what the circumstances are in the novel, I always imagine the characters are us. The difficult part is trying to keep my hands off Rory's creamy skin.

She comes into the bedroom with a towel wrapped around her body and another wrapped around her head. She heads for the dresser to get some clothes, but pajamas go against everything I have planned for her tonight. I leap out of bed and slide between her and the dresser.

"I'll go turn up the heater. No clothes is part of the deal."

She shakes her head as I set off into the hallway to turn up the heat. When I come back, she's gone. I peek into the bathroom and she's standing naked in front of the sink, brushing her hair. I enter behind her and take the brush from her hand. Her reflection smiles at mine and I continue brushing. I grab her towel off the rack to squeeze more water out of her hair, then I finish by blow-drying it.

Rory loves when I do girl stuff with her. I try not to imagine that this is because my sister isn't around to do this kind of stuff with her anymore, but it's hard not to. What's worse is that I actually enjoying blow-drying her hair and painting her nails because I know how happy it makes her. As long as she keeps her promise never to tell anyone I do these things, I'll probably be doing it for the rest of our lives.

I hang the blow-dryer on the rack she asked me to install in the bathroom last week for her hair tools. She turns around to face me and I just want to lift her up and slide my cock inside her right there, but I have to be patient tonight. Tonight is about the long game.

I grab her neck gently, placing my thumb over her pulse, then I kiss her tenderly until I can feel her heartbeat racing. Pulling away slowly, I place a soft kiss on her cheekbone before I take her hand and lead her into the bedroom. The book she bought today is lying on her side of the bed. I hold the covers up for her to get in, then I take off my boxers before sliding in next to her.

"Is this historical fiction?" I ask, as she settles in under the covers.

"I think it's—"

"Wait. Don't tell me. I want to try to figure it out."

"Of course. You like to be surprised." She drags out the "i" in "surprised" to mock me.

I reach over and gently grab her breast and she gasps because my hands are a little cold. "See? You like being surprised too."

She lightly smacks my hand. "All right. You've made your point. Can I have my breast back?"

"But it's so warm. Can I hold on a little longer? I promise I'll still listen."

She rolls her eyes as she begins reading the first page. "In the light of my grandmother's torchère, the one with the fringed lampshade, I wrote my first letter to my dead husband." She stops and slowly closes the book. "Maybe I should read something else."

"Why?"

She turns to me with tears glistening in the corners of her eyes. "I don't want to read this."

I let go of her breast and take the book from her hands. I lay it on my nightstand and by the time I turn back to her, she's composed herself. My hand slides under the sheet, quickly finding her soft abdomen. I brush the backs of my fingers over her skin as I slide my hand to her waist.

Burying my face in her neck, I whisper against her skin. "You want to tell me another story?"

She arches her back a little, pressing her chest to mine. "What kind of story?"

I slide my knee between her thighs as she coils her arms around my shoulders. "Your story."

She moans softly as I lightly dig my teeth into her neck. "My story is boring."

I suck on her neck and she wraps her legs around my hips. "Then tell me our story. Tell me how long you've wanted me." I slide my hand behind her knee and lift her leg so my erection is pressed against her throbbing pussy, but I don't enter her. "Then tell me how our story ends."

She squeezes her thighs together to tighten them around my hips and I gasp as my cock slides about an inch inside her. She grabs my face so she can look at me as I sink in slowly. Her eyelids flutter with ecstasy until I hit her cervix and she lets out a tiny gasp.

"Talk to me," I whisper as I move slowly in and out of her.

She smiles as she gently rakes her fingernails down my back, then back up to my shoulders, sending shivers through me and making my cock twitch. "The first time I saw you... you were on your skateboard."

I let out a soft chuckle, but she continues undaunted, as do I.

"You had your hat on backwards and... I think you were fourteen and you were already almost six feet tall. It was August and you were all sweaty."

I lift her left leg a bit higher so I can dig deeper. "You like it when I'm all sweaty?"

"Yes," she moans. "Yes... but I didn't realize I was in love with you until I was fifteen."

"Four... years... later?" I time my words with my thrusts and this makes her smile. "Why... so... long?"

She lets out a long sigh as I reach between her legs and massage her clit. "Because that's when I started touching myself."

"And you'd think of me?"

Her pussy clenches around my erection as I move my finger in slow circles around her swollen bud. She closes her eyes and tosses her head backward, exposing the graceful arch of her neck. The sensation of her muscles spasming around my dick is getting me too excited, so I pull out of her and her eyes flash open.

"Keep talking, baby," I urge her as I lay a hot trail of kisses down her neck all the way to her breasts.

She whimpers as I take her nipple into my mouth

and suck gently. "That was when you went away to college… I thought of you all the time and… I think I was touching myself at least once a day."

I tease her nipple with my tongue, smiling when she writhes a bit. "Is it wrong I find it hot you were fantasizing about me at that age?"

"Well, technically, you were eighteen and I was fifteen… so you would have been taking advantage of me if we actually did all the things I imagined we were doing."

My cock becomes painfully engorged at this comment. "Well, you're eighteen now, so tell me… what did you imagine us doing?"

I slide down and lay a soft kiss on her abdomen, then my head is between her legs. One of my favorite things about Rory is that she lets me shave her in the shower. Probably because she knows I'll make her come when I'm done. But nonetheless, it's one of my favorite parts of showering with her.

She draws in a sharp breath as I use my fingers to part her swollen lips, then I take her perfect clit into my mouth. "Oh, God, Houston."

"Keep talking or I'm gonna stop."

She laughs, but she quickly resumes her story. "This. This is what I used to imagine. And… I was a virgin, but I used to imagine you being my first."

"I *was* your first," I mutter, then I go back to licking her.

She threads her fingers through my hair, holding on for dear life as her legs begin to quiver. "I know… and it was *way* better than I imagined it would be."

I softly lick her up and down right at the one o'clock position on her clit and, as usual, she comes within seconds. I continue stimulating her, relishing the sound of her moans, until she grabs chunks of my hair and pulls me up.

I mash my lips to hers as I slide into her. I try to move slowly, but she grinds her hips into me, urging me on.

I pull back so I can look her in the eye. "Slow down, baby. The story's not over yet."

She smiles and pulls my mouth to hers again. Her kiss is hot and hungry, making it difficult for me to slow my pace, but I'm determined to make this last. I lift her leg again so she can watch my cock dipping in and out of her as I pierce her slowly and methodically.

Finally, she continues. "You know what comes after our first time together… What else do you want me to say?"

I pull out of her as my arms begin to shake. "Holy fuck. I'm getting so close to blowing my load. Give me a second."

"Holy fuck. I'm getting so close to blowing my load. Give me a second," she says, repeating my words back to me as if this is what I wanted her to say.

I laugh at her attempt to inject humor into the

situation, but it's not helping as my dick keeps twitching with an impending orgasm. "Don't move," I whisper, then I take a deep breath as I wait for the sensation to pass.

"Okay, I'll just keep talking. You wanted to know how our story ends?"

I look up at her and she smiles as I very slowly ease my cock back inside her. "How does it end?"

She gazes into my eyes for a moment before she responds. "It doesn't have to end, does it?"

Unable to hold back any longer, I press my lips together to keep from grunting as I come inside her. Then I think of how our relationship began and how I've always known that it's going to end.

I lay a soft kiss on the corner of her lips. "I hope it never ends."

Rory

Five years ago, February 14th

HOUSTON IS GONE by the time I wake up Saturday morning. Our first Valentine's Day together. Or *not* together, I guess. I forgot about Valentine's Day while I was with Houston last night. I don't know if that's a testament to how much I love him or how good he is at making me forget that anything and anyone else exists.

I consider lying in bed and wallowing for the rest of the day, but I know I'll start thinking about Hallie and I'll be a crying mess before long. I should go back to Barnes & Noble and find a more uplifting book, but uplifting is not exactly better. I finally decide to just get up and go for a run.

By the time I have my running shoes and yellow

fleece jacket on, Houston bursts through the front door soaked from head to toe and shivering.

"What happened to you?" I ask as I rush over to help him out of his UO hoodie. The rainwater soaking his clothes is so frigid, the cold penetrates through my fleece jacket. "You have to get out of those clothes. You're freezing. What were you doing out there?"

He pushes my hands away to stop me from removing his hoodie. "Stop, stop. You need to come outside."

"Are you crazy? You need to change your clothes."

He smiles. "We can do that later. Right now, you need to come outside with me. But grab an umbrella."

I shake my head as I grab an umbrella out of the stand next to the door. "You're acting weird."

He leads me through the courtyard and out to the parking lot. The freezing rain batters the top of my umbrella, but Houston doesn't bother trying to take shelter with me. He doesn't even flinch as the rain batters his hulking shoulders, as if he's a god impervious to the elements.

Where Houston's truck should be parked under the carport, I spot another car, a brand-new silver Prius tied with a soggy red bow. That's why he was parked on the street last night?

"What the fuck is that?"

He laughs as he pulls me toward the car. "It's yours. The ribbon got a little wet while I was tying it. Do you know how hard it is to tie a ribbon on a car in the middle of a rainstorm?"

"The *ribbon* got wet?" I reply, looking him up and down. "You're insane."

"I'm in love. It kinda goes with the territory. Happy Valentine's Day."

In love? Houston has never told me he loves me. This is the first time he's hinted at it. Well, I guess buying me a car is also a pretty huge hint. I want to scream *I love you!* loud enough for it to echo in a neighboring galaxy, but I'm speechless.

The hand holding my umbrella falls to my side and raindrops fall steadily on my cheeks. I drop the umbrella and stand on my tiptoes so I can throw my arms around his neck. He squats down and wraps his arms around the tops of my thighs, then he lifts me up so I'm about six inches taller than him.

I cradle his beautiful face in my hands and kiss him with such ferocity our teeth clack against each other. We both chuckle, then I slow down a little so I can savor the sensation of his warm tongue brushing against mine. The rain taps the back of my head, slithering through my hair, then down our faces. I turn my head to catch my breath and Houston sets me down gently.

"You're shaking. I'm taking you inside." He grabs my hand and sets off toward the courtyard, but I dig my heels into the asphalt.

"Wait! I didn't get you anything."

He turns back to me, confused. "Yes, you did. You told me a story."

"But… I'm sorry. I can't accept the car. I don't deserve it." My protests are slightly garbled by the staticky sound of rain pouring all around us.

"What are you talking about? Of course you do. And, no offense, but your car is a piece of shit. You need this car."

A green SUV pulls into the lot and Houston pulls me aside so we're under the carport.

I wipe the rain from my face and eyelashes. "But what happens if we break up? I can't afford to make a car payment with a part-time minimum-wage job. That's why you took me in. I'm poor."

"That's not why I took you in."

I flash him my best *don't-even-try-to-bullshit-me-right-now* expression.

He laughs. "Okay, fine. That *is* partially why I took you in, but the important thing is that we're not going to break up. The story never ends, remember?"

"Houston, that was a story. It's not real life. In real life, shit happens."

He lets out an impatient sigh. "Fine. If it makes you feel better, you can keep your old car in case we break up."

"But where are we gonna keep it? *Oh!* I can keep it in the garage at home. Can you follow me home in your truck—or better yet, follow me in the new car so I can show my parents?"

He's silent for a moment as he contemplates my request, then he smiles. "I can't. I promised Troy we'd go to the game tomorrow. But I'll buy you a train ticket for the ride back. Go visit your parents, on me."

I consider whining to get my way, because I really want my parents to see my new car. And I really, really want them to see me with Houston, to see how happy we are together. So they can see there is still one bright spark of hope in my life. But he did just buy me a car. I can't be too demanding right now.

I reach for him and he leans down so I can wrap my arms around his solid neck. "Thank you, from the bottom of my heart, for taking me in. And for giving me a fucking car."

He laughs as he tilts his head back so he can kiss the tip of my nose.

"But most of all," I continue, "thanks for being my friend. I... I..."

He squeezes me harder, and for the first time since we left the apartment I feel warm. "I love you more," he whispers in my ear. "But all I ask in return for this car is that you let me tie you up tonight."

"I knew there was a catch." I grin stupidly as the words *I love you more* repeat inside my mind like a beautifully broken record.

He slides his hand underneath my jacket and I flinch a little when his icy fingers whisper over the small of my back. "There's always a catch."

Part 2: Anger

"We're all searching for
someone whose demons
play well with ours."
-*Anonymous*

Houston

Six years ago, December 24ᵗʰ

CHRISTMAS EVE IS usually the day I'm reminded of how my father's affair tore our family to shreds. Hallie and I normally spend the day commiserating over our mutual dislike of our stepmother, Ilsa, while also expressing how glad we are that we'll never have to spend another Christmas with her family again—not after the scene Hallie and I caused during our first post-divorce holiday dinner.

I grab a bottle of Hallie's favorite sparkling cranberry juice out of the fridge and head toward the dining room. As I make my way around the corner, I can already hear her voice, bubbly and sweet as the contents of the bottle in my hand, chatting with Rory and my mom. Rory must have just arrived. I consider going back to the kitchen to grab something for her to drink, but I don't really know what beverage she prefers with her Christmas dinner. This is the first time Rory will be spending Christmas Eve with us.

I'm not supposed to know that Rory has a crush on me, but it's kind of hard not to notice the way she quickly turns away whenever I look at her. Or the way it takes her a few seconds to compose herself whenever I answer the phone or the front door.

Also, last year, Hallie confessed that Rory has had a crush on me for a long time, though she won't tell me how long. I don't think Hallie meant to betray Rory's trust by telling me this. It's just really hard for Hallie and me to keep anything from each other. Considering Hallie told me about Rory's crush more than a year ago, it's possible she's over it by now, especially since it's been about sixteen months since I left McMinnville for UO.

I enter the dining room and stop in the middle of the archway when I see Rory bent over the table arranging the silverware. She's wearing a short-sleeved, curve-hugging sweater dress the color of fresh milk. The dress is cut just above her knees, exposing her fair skin, which looks just as soft and creamy. A fiery longing ignites my insides as I'm unable to tear my gaze from her perfect ass.

How have I never noticed that body?

"Uh… Houston, we have a problem?"

I turn sideways and find Hallie standing right at my left, her eyebrows raised. "What?" I shake my head to clear the image of Rory, then I hold up the bottle of cranberry juice. "What do you mean? This isn't what you wanted?"

My eyes flit back to Rory, but she's on the other side of the table helping my mom open a bottle of wine. Now I have a view of her from the front and it's even better, if that's possible. The dress clings to the swell of her breasts and the curve of her hips, accentuating her hourglass figure.

When did Rory grow up?

Suddenly, Hallie yanks me by the arm until we're outside of the dining room, out of Rory and Mom's line of sight. Her blue eyes bore into me, seeking answers. But I stare back at her, pretending not to know what she wants.

"What was that?" she demands.

"What?"

She tilts her head. "Don't play dumb with me, Huey."

I scrunch my nose at the sound of my mom's old nickname for me. Hallie only uses it when she wants to get something out of me. She knows I'll cave just so I don't have to hear it anymore.

"I was just looking. Don't worry. I know she's off limits."

She looks confused by this statement. "What do you

mean, she's off limits? I don't care if you get with Rory. You know that."

"It's not that. She's off limits because she's seventeen."

I don't say it aloud, but it's pretty much the duty of every man over eighteen to know the age of consent in their state. In Oregon, the age of consent is eighteen. I'm twenty. Rory is seventeen. She's off limits.

"That's so lame," Hallie replies, rolling her eyes. "Rory would do backflips if you stuck your wiener in her. She wouldn't go to the cops."

I shake my head. "Yeah, I'm not having this conversation with you. Besides, if she did backflips when I stuck my dick in her, I'm pretty sure *I'd* be the one calling the cops."

She curls her lip at this reply. "Yeah, I don't need that kind of visual right before we eat."

"You started it."

She takes the bottle of sparkling juice from my hand and we both head into the dining room together. My mom is pulling her dark hair up into a ponytail as Rory pours her a glass of wine.

"Geez, what temperature is the thermostat set at. It's hotter than Satan's waiting room in here."

Hallie sets her juice on the table and takes a seat. "How do you know Satan's a doctor?"

My mom fans her face with one hand as she grabs her glass of red wine with the other. "Someone turn down the heater."

"It's just a hot flash, Mom," I say, trying not to look at Rory as I take the seat between her and Hallie at the round dining table.

"*Just* a hot flash? Well, now it'll be *just* a little cold. You can put on your Christmas sweater."

I try not to laugh as I get up from the table to adjust the thermostat.

Hallie holds her hand out to stop me. "I'll turn it down. I have to show Rory something in my room really quick, anyway." She looks at Rory and nods toward the corridor, but Rory looks confused. "Come on."

Rory shrugs and flashes my mom an adorable smile as she gets up from the table. I don't bother trying not to look at her as she walks away. It's just my mom in here now, and she's too busy holding the cold bottle of juice against her cheek to notice.

When Hallie and Rory return a few minutes later, I search their faces for any sign that Hallie may have told Rory about how she caught me ogling her. But Rory appears as uncomfortable around me as she always does, looking everywhere but at me as she smooths her dress and takes a seat in her chair. I find myself wondering what kind of bra and panties she has on underneath that dress. Or if she's wearing any at all. Just the thought of that makes my cock twitch.

I need to get this under control. Too bad I'm not twenty-one, or I'd be pouring myself a glass of red wine to dull these unexpected urges. Though I'm pretty sure my mom knows I drink, I know she won't condone it in her house. Besides, getting a drink or two in me might actually backfire.

We each take turns passing around the mashed potatoes, string beans, maple-glazed carrots, and the tray piled high with sliced turkey smothered in gravy, until our plates are overflowing with food. Every time Rory passes me a dish, I look her in the eye to keep from staring at the way her dark red hair falls softly over her cleavage. As we eat, I find myself stealing glances at her, watching the fork as it disappears inside her mouth, her lips wrapped tightly around the steel before it comes out clean again.

Hallie clears her throat. "Ahem. So Houston, how's that new business coming along?"

I narrow my eyes at Hallie. She knows Mom doesn't know about my little side business. I don't know what she's getting at by bringing this up now.

My mom looks up from her plate. "What is she talking about, Hugh? I haven't heard anything about this."

Hallie smiles. "Oh, it's nothing. Troy and Houston are brewing non-alcoholic beer."

I look at her like she's crazy, but she just smiles and continues.

"Yeah, they named their company Barley Legal. Isn't that cute? *Barley* Legal." She looks very pleased with herself as Rory covers her mouth to keep from laughing. "Get it? Because it's non-alcoholic beer, so it's legal for him to make it and to drink it. Pretty cool, huh? I think Houston's going places with that one."

I shake my head at her. "You're insane, but I still love you."

"Ew, Mom. He loves me. Tell him to stop."

My mom rolls her eyes. "Oh, you two, that's enough. Finish your food so we can open presents. I'm sure Rory's dying to get back to her normal family."

"That's not true," Hallie replies as she stabs her fork into a string bean. "Rory loves our crazy family. Don't you, Rory?"

Rory glances at me then goes back to staring at her plate of food. "Yes, I do. Almost as much as I love... Um..."

"Don't hurt yourself," Hallie says with a wink of her eye. "The word you're looking for is turkey. You love us almost as much as you love turkey. Right?"

Rory nods as she presses her full lips together, trying not to smile. She's wearing red lipstick today, which accentuates her fiery auburn hair. Everything about her looks different. I don't think she normally wears enough makeup for anyone to notice. I normally prefer the girls I date to look naturally beautiful, but if Rory hadn't worn that red lipstick and that white dress today, I may never have noticed her.

What the fuck am I am thinking? I can't date Rory.

I shake my head as I mentally cross her name off my to-do list.

When we're done eating, Rory offers to do the dishes, the way she always does when she has dinner at our house. But this time, I offer to help her instead of sitting back and letting Hallie do it. My sister cocks an eyebrow at me as she and Mom walk out of the kitchen to start sorting the presents in the living room.

When I turn around, Rory is already washing the large roasting pan my mom used for the turkey. I place my hand gently on her arm and she flinches. Her gaze is fixed on the sudsy water in the pan as she waits for me to say something.

"I'm sorry. I didn't mean to startle you," I say, gently taking the pan out of her hands. "I'll wash, you dry. I don't want—I mean—you don't want to get your dress dirty."

She smiles as she rinses the soap off her hands, then she steps aside and grabs a clean dish towel out of a drawer. We spend the next five minutes in relative silence. I pretend to care whether every bit of grease comes off every dish, drawing out the moment until I can work up the nerve to say something to her. She alternates between crossing her arms, biting her lip, and staring at the floor. Finally, I get an idea.

I finish rinsing my mom's wine glass, but when I reach out to give it to her, I pretend to accidentally drop it. "Shit!"

"Oh, no!" Rory says, immediately squatting down to clean it up, giving me a spectacular view of her ass.

It takes me a moment to tear my gaze away from her body, then I kneel next to her, reaching for her towel. "I'll clean it up. It was my mistake."

She stares at my hand on hers and seems unable to speak. I gently ease the towel out of her grip and she finally looks up at me. I flash her a warm smile and she looks confused. It takes a moment, but she seems to get her bearings and quickly stands up, leaving a soft cloud of vanilla-scented air in her wake. I sigh as I breathe in the fragrance while cleaning up the glass.

"You can go ahead," I say, as I carry the jagged shards to the trash bin. "I'll finish up in here."

I'm drying the last few pieces of silverware when Hallie comes into the kitchen. She crosses her arms and tilts her head, waiting for me to say something.

"What?"

"That's how it starts," she says. "First, you try looking for ways to be around them. Even doing shitty stuff like washing the dishes seems fun if it means you get to spend one moment with them."

I place the forks in the utensil drawer and cock an eyebrow. "Are you speaking from experience? I don't seem to remember you bringing any guys around here."

"What makes you think I'd bring a guy I like around you?"

I slide the drawer shut and lean back against the

counter. "It's not what you think it is. She just… She looks different today."

"Yep, that's how it started for me, too. You have to tell her, Houston. Don't be a pussy."

I laugh as I shake my head. "No fuckin' way. She's not old enough. If I still feel the same when she's eighteen, I'll think about it."

A dull sadness washes over her features. "Fine."

She turns around and heads back to the living room. I wait a moment before I follow after her. When I enter the room, I find Rory sitting on the sofa with a pile of presents at her feet. Hallie hands her the gifts one at a time and Rory shakes each box to try to guess what's inside before she places it on the cushion next to her.

Hallie holds up a long, thin box and reads the gift tag. "From Hallie to Rory," she says, handing Rory the box. "You don't have to bother shaking that one. It's your new battery-operated boyfriend."

My mom's jaw drops. "Hallie, you didn't."

"Oh, yes I did, Mom. And I got you one, too."

Rory and I burst into hysterics. She whips her head around at the sound of my laughter and quickly tries to hide the long box behind the other presents on the sofa.

"Oh, my God," she mutters, covering her face with her hands.

I try to keep from laughing even more at her embarrassment as I make my way toward the sofa. Sitting down on the opposite end so Rory's presents form a barrier between us, I hold out my hand for Hallie to give me my first gift.

"To Houston from Hallie," she says proudly.

I take the shirt-sized box wrapped in green paper from her hand, and sure enough I can feel the soft weight of some type of clothing sliding around inside. "Is this the butt-plug I asked for?"

She shakes her head. "Can't sneak anything past you."

I wink at Rory as I set the box down next to her vibrator. "She knows me so well."

My mom sighs as she yanks the hair-tie out of her hair and plops down onto the recliner on the other side of the Christmas tree. "How did I raise such twisted children? Where did I go wrong?"

Hallie pats my mom's knee. "Don't worry, Mom. It's the kids that are too afraid to have the butt-plug conversation with their parents who end up in trouble."

"That's very reassuring," my mom replies.

Once Hallie has sorted the presents by recipient, we all open our gifts at the same time. This is the tradition in our home ever since Mom and Dad divorced. My mom felt the need to change all the traditions that reminded her too much of my father, which is also why we celebrate Christmas on Christmas Eve now instead of Christmas Day.

Hallie helps Rory stuff her five gifts into a couple of grocery tote bags so she can carry them back to the house. But she leaves the unopened vibrator box behind. Hallie joins me in the living room to clean up the boxes and wrapping paper while my mom puts a couple of logs in the fireplace.

I grab a couple of Rory's discarded boxes and stuff them into the large trash bag Hallie's carrying. "That wasn't so bad."

"Speak for yourself. You really confused Rory."

"What's wrong with Rory?" my mom asks as she grabs the lighter off the mantle.

My stomach clenches at the thought that I may have made Rory uncomfortable or confused. "I guess I should just back off."

"Or you could, you know, follow through and ask her if she has any plans for New Year's Eve."

I take the trash bag from Hallie. "No, I'll just wait it out. These things pass."

She sighs as she stares at my mom with a far-off look in her eyes. "Like I said, speak for yourself."

"What does that mean?"

She shakes her head and grabs another piece of torn wrapping paper off the carpet. "It's not that easy. True love doesn't disappear with time."

"Are you saying Rory is in love with me?" My heart races at this thought, but I can't decide if I'm more excited or scared.

"I don't know. Just forget it. It's probably best if you two don't hook up. I don't want you getting between me and Rory."

"Are you trying to set your brother up with Rory?" my mom calls over her shoulder as she pokes the small fire in the grate. "That's a dangerous situation, Hallie. You have to be prepared to accept the consequences if it doesn't work out."

Hallie sinks down onto the sofa cushion. "I just want everyone to be happy. Love makes people happy."

My mom shakes her head. "Love can also make you crazy and miserable. Don't forget that."

Hallie sighs as I take a seat next to her, then she rests her head on my shoulder. "And I'll bet it's totally worth it."

Houston

August 24th

I GET UP an hour earlier so I can get out of the apartment before Tessa wakes. I grab a light rain jacket. It's one of those rare August days in Portland where the rain clouds roll in and attempt to dampen everyone's summer plans. Not that anyone in Portland can be deterred by a smattering of rain. I'm almost out the front door when Tessa stumbles out of the bedroom, squinting at me through the gray morning light.

"Why are you leaving so early?"

I'm tempted to tell her that it's none of her business. That she lost the privilege to question me when she betrayed me by getting pregnant behind my back. That she never really earned the privilege to question me because our whole relationship has been teetering on a knife-edge waiting for something exactly like this to happen.

Picturing the two of us careening off the edge reminds me of a quote I read in college: *This is the way we fall. First we lose our balance, teetering precariously on the edge of uncertainty, until, mercilessly, gravity takes over. You can't outshine gravity.* Tessa and I are about to topple over and she's either too stubborn to admit it or too delusional to see it.

"I'm heading to work early."

"But, we didn't get to talk about…"

"About what? If you're truly pregnant, you need to get an abortion."

"Abortion?" she shrieks, her face contorted with disbelief. "I'm not getting an *abortion*. How can you even *suggest* that?"

I step back inside the apartment and push the door closed. "How can I suggest that? What else do you propose we do? Raise a child in a home built on lies? Is that what you want for your child?"

"*Our* child. And it's not a lie if I told you the truth. I didn't hide the pregnancy from you."

"No, you just lied about being on birth control. So where are the test results? How do I know you're really pregnant? Am I supposed to take your word for it? Because right now your word holds zero value with me."

"Why do you hate me? Is it because I'm not *her*?"

"I don't even know what you're talking about," I reply, in no mood to listen to more accusations of adultery.

I cheated on her one time before we were engaged and I'll never live it down. I wish Tessa knew how fucking badly I want to cheat on her with Rory right now and how her accusations only serve to chip away at my loyalty even further.

Loyalty. You'd think I'd know the meaning of the word since I have it tattooed across my chest. But it seems the older I get, the line between loyalty and treachery becomes thinner and blurrier.

Marriage is not simple. I knew that going into it. But there are all types of betrayal in a marriage, and most of them don't involve adultery.

I turn to leave and she rushes to my side.

Latching on to my arm, her face is wrought with fear. "Wait. I'm sorry. I didn't mean that. Don't go. Please. We can talk about this."

My stomach vaults at her desperation. "I have to go to work." I try to wrench my arm out of her grasp, but she tightens her grip. "Let go, Tessa."

She shakes her head. "No. Come to bed." She reaches for my face and I flinch.

"Stop it."

Her hand slides down and I look her straight in the eye as she curls her fingers around the bulge in my jeans.

"Don't do this, Tessa. Let it go."

She moves her hand up and down, stroking me through my pants. "Fuck me, Houston."

I grit my teeth and will myself not to get an erection. How is it that my wife's touch makes me feel as if I'm cheating on Rory?

I look her in the eye as I push her away. "I'd rather fuck my hand."

Her eyes widen in utter disbelief. "I'm leaving." She storms away toward the bedroom. "I'm going to my mother's. At least she'll miss me when I'm gone."

I want to roll my eyes and call her bluff, but I can't. I knew a guy named Greg in high school, a friend of a friend, who used to threaten to commit suicide whenever his girlfriend, Alisha, was on the brink of dumping him. It worked for about three years, until Alisha finally called Greg's bluff. He ended up in the hospital that night after taking thirty Tylenol. Any asshole with half a brain knows thirty Tylenol won't do anything to a healthy person, except maybe make you vomit or possibly pass out. Alisha didn't visit Greg in the hospital and he got himself a new girlfriend a few months later. If Greg was the only example of attempted suicide following a breakup I've ever come across in all my twenty-seven years, I would totally call Tessa's bluff.

I follow her into the bedroom and find she has two magenta suitcases open on the bed. Her clothes fly haphazardly out of her dresser drawers and somehow most of them find their way inside her luggage.

"Tessa." I call her name from where I stand in the safety of the doorway. "Tessa, look at me."

"Why?" she wails, her voice thick with tears. "You've been trying to get rid of me since before we even got married. This is what you wanted, isn't it?"

"What are you talking about? I never tried to get rid of you."

She rounds on me, clutching a bundle of panties to her chest. "You never loved me, did you? All that stuff about *my pain is your pain* and all that other crap was just bullshit. Wasn't it? You don't give a damn about me or what I've gone through." She lifts her left arm to show me the scars on the inside of her forearm. "You don't care how I got these. You've never even asked. You probably even think I'm bluffing when I say I'll kill myself."

"Don't say that. Just… don't even say it."

"Why? You don't want to be responsible for another suicide?"

Her words spark a jolt of violent rage within me. "Shut up! Shut your *fucking* mouth! You don't know what the fuck you're talking about."

She's stunned for a moment, then her lips begin to tremble. "I'm sorry." She whispers this a few more times as she sinks down to the floor. "Please don't make me go."

I take a few steps closer and find her sitting on the carpet near the foot of the bed. "Make you go where?

You're the one who said you were leaving."

"I don't want to leave." She looks up, her blonde hair sticking out in all directions as her eyes plead with me. "I'll get an abortion. I'll see a therapist. I'll do anything. Just please don't leave me." She sobs as she grasps chunks of her hair. "I don't... I don't... I don't know who I am without you."

I stare at her for a moment, trying to hold on to the anger and disgust I felt a moment ago, but I can't. I sink down next to her and take her into my arms, where she sobs heavily for a while. And as I stroke her hair and wait for her to finish, I wonder how long Rory will wait to find out what's inside that box.

Rory

I TAKE MY time walking to my new workplace on Burnside, turning a seven-minute walk into a ten-minute leisurely stroll. The contents of the Sierra Nevada tin box are clinking around inside my backpack. It sounds like a ring, but I refuse to peek inside. If Houston would rather present it to me himself, he must have a good reason. And I'm pretty certain he knows I have no desire to be his mistress. Maybe whatever's in the box is a sign that he's leaving his wife.

Is that what I want? Do I want to be responsible for breaking up a marriage? Would it be fair to call me a home-wrecker if I haven't actually had an affair with Houston and *he* was the one who pursued me?

I don't know the answers to any of these questions. All I know is that I do miss Houston. He was my first love, my default best friend after Hallie died, my protector and provider, and, for a split second, the father of my unborn child. Of course I miss him and everything we had. That doesn't mean that we belong together.

I enter the Zucker's on Burnside through the front and my gaze lands on the plastic sheeting on my right. Behind the semi-transparent veil, people are moving inside the coffee bar. A signpost standing in front of the plastic shroud reads: Excuse our dust. New Zucker's Café & Wine Bar coming soon!

I look left and spot a door behind the customer service counter, which must lead to an office. Jamie told me to ask for the store's general manager, Benji. A blonde cashier spots my green Zucker's T-shirt as she's bagging some produce for a customer. She flashes me a warm smile and I return it.

"Is that Benji's office?" I ask her, pointing at the door behind the customer service counter.

She nods. "Yep. He's in there right now."

"Thanks."

I slip behind the counter and knock on the door. A few seconds pass before a guy's face appears behind the small window set into the door at eye level. I can't see him very well through the wire mesh between the window panes, but he looks pretty young to be a general manager.

The door opens inward and Benji smiles at me. "Are you Aurora?"

"Yeah, but everyone calls me Rory."

He motions to a chair. "Well, have a seat, Rory, and I'll get you up to speed. I'm Benji Zucker, by the way."

I try to focus as Benji explains the job to me, but all I can think is that Grandpa Zucker must really trust his young grandkids to give them such powerful positions in the company. Benji is very friendly, which makes me think he was born, or bred, to do this kind of job. He doesn't patronize me when he explains the magnitude of my new responsibilities. He turns his computer screen toward me so he can give me a tutorial on the new inventory system they implemented a few weeks ago. When he explains the tasks associated with vendor management, my eyes glaze over as I imagine trying to "manage" a relationship with Houston's company.

"Rory?"

I blink a few times and smile. "Yes. Sorry, I got a little distracted. I was just thinking about the vendor management stuff. Does that entail meeting with vendors *in person* or would it just be phone meetings?"

He looks confused by my question. "Do you have an issue meeting with vendors?"

"No, no. I'm just, as you can tell, a bit awkward in person. I'm much better on the phone. But I have no problem meeting with vendors in person. I was just curious." The skeptical look on his face tells me he's not buying it. "I swear, I'm fine. I promise I'll do a good job. You have nothing to worry about."

He nods as he dials a number on his desk phone. I have a weird fantasy that he's calling security to have me hauled out of here. This makes me grin and he smiles back at me.

"Bella, can you come get Rory from my office? She's ready for you." He sets the phone down on the cradle and smiles as he turns his computer monitor around so I can't see the screen anymore. "Bella is the manager of the wine bar, but she's four months pregnant. You're going to have to pay close attention to what she does so you can take over when she goes on leave in five months. Do you think you can handle that?"

"Absolutely."

He nods as he types something, then he pushes his keyboard aside and looks me in the eye. "I heard you're a writer."

This catches me off-guard. I've only mentioned my writing to Jamie once. I don't know what that has to do with anything.

"Uh… I write sometimes. Not sure I'd call that being a *writer*."

"But you know how to write? Like, you know the basic rules of grammar and stuff, right?"

I chuckle. "Yeah, I hope so. I have a bachelor's in English."

"Cool. I might have a project for you that involves

writing."

"A work project?"

He flashes me a sheepish grin. "It's a personal project. I… need help writing my wedding vows and Jamie recommended you. Is that okay? Obviously, you don't need to do it if you're not comfortable with it."

"Yeah, totally. Anything I can do to help."

"Cool. I'm getting married in three weeks and I'm shitting bricks over these vows."

I open my mouth to reply, but I'm interrupted by a knock at the door. I stand quickly and begin smoothing down my T-shirt as if we've been caught doing something naughty. Bella is a tall, doe-eyed brunette with ample breasts and a small baby bump. Her perfectly understated makeup makes me feel a bit self-conscious about my lack of makeup. If a pregnant woman can take the time to look that good, I have no excuse not to.

Bella holds out her hand for me to shake. "I'm Bella." She pats her belly, then glances at Benji. "And this little guy in here is Benjamin Jr."

I turn to Benji and he's grinning from ear to ear. "Bella and I are getting married in three weeks."

I swallow hard as I realize I just agreed to write wedding vows for *both* of my bosses' weddings. *Great!*

BELLA AND I spend a couple of hours in the stockroom updating inventory for use with the new software. All the while dodging construction workers who scurry back and forth from the warehouse to the stockroom then to the bar area, installing supply cabinets, patching drywall, connecting the plumbing for three different sinks. I make it through the first couple of hours of inventory management with ease. Then Bella informs me we have a city building inspector coming in at two p.m. to inspect the coolers in the basement where the draft beer will be stored. And a beer vendor is coming in to oversee the inspection. We work in silence a bit longer, scanning boxes of coffee syrup, tea, and coffee stirrers into the computer system, but my curiosity soon gets the best of me.

"So, this guy who's coming to oversee the inspection... what company is he with?"

Bella chuckles, but she doesn't look away from the box she's scanning. "It's called Barley Legal. I think it's a cute name. And the guy's über hot, too. Maybe you could, you know?" She sticks out her chest and jiggles her boobs a little. "Unless you're not single, then disregard my advice."

Heat rises into my cheeks, but I can't tell if I'm blushing because she's complimenting my ex-boyfriend or if I'm flushing with jealousy because she called him über hot. Either way, I need to figure out how I'm going to approach the situation when Houston gets here. Do I let him go about his business and pretend I don't know him? Do I opt for honesty and tell Bella he's my ex? Maybe the honest approach will help me get closer to Bella and get to know her better. Then I'll be better equipped to help Benji write his vows.

Of course, getting in good with the boss is positive for my working environment, but how long do I actually plan to work here? The plan is to eventually make my living as a writer, isn't it? That was the point of changing my major after Houston and I broke up, wasn't it?

I shake my head as I scan a case of cinnamon syrup. Maybe I just want to stick my flag in Houston, claim him as mine again, if only in the past tense. That's so pathetic.

On cue, my phone buzzes in my pocket and I quickly retrieve it, heart pounding as I imagine it's Houston with his promise to show me the contents of the box when he comes in. But it's not Houston. It's Liam, with a text that makes me laugh so loud Bella drops her scanner gun.

Liam: *In the most boring meeting of my life and thinking, this would be less boring if Rory and her ex-boyfriend were here.*

Bella picks up the scanner gun and stares at me. "Well? What's the joke?"

I shake my head. "It's totally lame. Sort of an inside

joke."

"I wouldn't get it?"

"Ugh. I hate when people say that, but it's actually true. Here, you can read it."

I hold my phone out with the screen pointed at her.

"So this guy, Liam," she begins, not looking particularly impressed, "I take it the last time you two hooked up, your ex-boyfriend showed up and decked him, or you had a threesome. Which is it?"

I laugh as I stare at the text. "No violence or sex involved, but everything else is correct."

She moves toward the door leading out to the warehouse. "No violence or sex? That must be a *really* boring meeting he's in."

I follow her into the warehouse and she takes me down to the basement, where the walk-in cooler was installed yesterday. She introduces me to a few stock boys along the way, waggling her eyebrows when one of the better-looking ones glances repeatedly at my boobs. Finally, we make it down to the cooler, which is installed below the wine bar. A notice on the steel door has the name of the company and the man who installed the cooler, the company phone number, and the date of the installation.

"Wait right here so you can greet the inspector when he comes down. That way I can stay up there in case any of those guys need anything."

"But I don't know anything about inspections or

coolers."

"You don't have to. That's why the Barley Legal dude and the installer are coming at the same time. They'll talk to the inspector. You're here in case they need a manager to sign off on something."

I open my mouth to remind her that I'm not a manager, but I stop before I can make a fool of myself. "Got it. I'll just wait here."

Once Bella is gone, I pull my phone out of my pocket again to respond to Liam. It takes me seven excruciating minutes to come up with something remotely clever.

Me: *I hope your next visit is less traumatic.*

Liam: *Next visit? Are you hitting on me? Don't answer that. I accept. I'll be there at 8.*

I laugh as I tuck the phone back into my pocket. When I look up, I nearly jump out of my skin at the sight of Troy Bingham, Houston's best friend through high school and college. They must run Barley Legal together. Is this the über hot guy Bella was referring to?

His blue eyes are bright with excitement. "Rory? Are you shitting me? Holy fuck. Look at you, girl."

He holds his arms out for me to give him a hug. I give him a quick pat-on-the-back type of hug, but he holds on a few seconds longer than expected. He lets go and looks me up and down a couple of times, shaking his head.

"Houston told me he ran into you, but I didn't really believe it. I mean, what are the fuckin' odds, you working here while we're setting this up?"

"Houston told you he ran into me?"

"Yeah, of course. He couldn't keep that to himself. You know how crazy he was about you."

My hands begin to shake, so I tuck them behind my back. "So... you're here for the inspection?"

"Oh, yeah. You probably thought Houston was coming. He was supposed to, but he had some kind of emergency at home. I think there's trouble in paradise, if you know what I mean."

Is Troy trying to convince me to have an affair with Houston?

"I don't really know," I reply, unable to disguise the tremor in my voice. "I don't know Houston anymore."

"What are you talking about? Houston's the same guy he always was, just richer."

"And married-er."

He shrugs as he chuckles. "If you can call it a marriage. Whatever. None of my business."

"Or mine."

"That's debatable."

"Excuse me?"

He waves off the comment. "Nothing. I was only kidding. So where's the inspector?"

I draw in a deep breath to calm my nerves. "I was told he would be here at the same time as you and the installer. I don't really know. This is my first day at this store."

"I guess we'll just wait, then." He smiles as he tucks his hands into his jeans pockets and leans back against the steel door. "Rory, can you do me a favor?"

"What kind of favor?"

"Can you not tell Houston what I said about his marriage? The thing is… He spoke to me about you in confidence and, to be totally fucking honest, I've never liked his wife. I guess I let my personal feelings about her get away from me. I shouldn't have said that stuff about his marriage being on the rocks. I don't know if that's true."

I'm silent for a moment as I try to remember what it was like not to want Houston. I wish I could call him right now and ask him if there's any truth to Troy's assertions. What kind of emergency at home kept him from coming here today? Did something happen to his wife? Did she find out about his visit to my apartment last night?

Or maybe Houston just didn't want to see me today.

"No worries," I say, leaning against the door. "Anyway, Houston's marriage is none of my business."

After a stiff, awkward silence, Troy turns to me and smiles. "But I wasn't lying when I said he was crazy about you… And if you ask me, he still is."

Rory

August 24ᵗʰ

AFTER MY FIRST day as the assistant manager of the former coffee bar slash soon-to-be wine-slash-coffee bar, Benji sends me off with a worn, folded sheet of paper containing his best intentions. I'm tempted to read his attempt at wedding vows on the walk home, but I'm afraid the light rain will ruin the thin, worn paper. The moment I walk inside my apartment, my mom greets me at the door with Skippy. The salacious grin on her face is a bit frightening.

I set my backpack containing Benji's vows and the Sierra Nevada box on the breakfast bar and crouch down to smooch Skippy. His tongue makes a loud clopping noise as he laps my face, his tail wagging so hard his whole butt shimmies from side to side. Holding my arms out for a hug, I smile when he lays his paws on my shoulders like a good pup. Then I squeeze him hard, burying my nose in his black fur as he whines and continues to lick my cheek and ear.

"I know, buddy. I missed you, too." I let him go and get to my feet, trying to ignore the backpack as I make my way into the kitchen. "Did you check his blood glucose? And why are you so happy?"

My mom follows closely behind me. "Yes, I did, twenty minutes ago. He's fine for now. And I heard you had a man here last night. Actually, *two* men."

I roll my eyes as I imagine Mrs. Vernor from across the hall standing inside her door last night, listening to what was going on in the corridor. Then she took it upon herself to pass the juicy gossip onto my mom today.

"It was nothing. Just a couple of friends."

"Since when do you have boyfriends?"

"Not boyfriends. Just friends who happen to be guys."

I pour myself a glass of water from the tap and gulp it down, leaving the glass in the sink to use it later. As expected, my mom pushes me aside so she can wash it now. She hates the sight of dirty dishes in the sink.

"Don't play coy with me, Rory. And don't be so secretive. It's good to talk about your love life. It helps you work out problems you might not be able to work out on your own."

"Who says I'm having problems? And who says I have a love life?"

"Well, you're going to have to work pretty hard to maintain a love life if you bottle everything up."

For a moment, I consider telling my mom everything that happened last night with Houston and Liam. Then I remember how much she hated Houston after he broke my heart. She may have been a strict grammarian during her days as a schoolteacher, but she threw all the rules of language out the window when she spoke of him during that time. Of course, it probably had to do with the fact that she was so stressed over the divorce at the time. She was on a man-hating kick for a while there.

"Why are you so concerned with me getting a boyfriend? It's been five years since you and dad divorced and you're still single."

"That's different. I'm old. I've done the whole marriage, career, family thing. I can take my time finding my next partner."

I shake my head as I head for the bedroom with Skippy and my mom trailing right behind. "That's such a load of crap, Mom. If anything, being old means you have *less* time to find your next partner. I'm the one who can take my time. I'm twenty-four. I have at least fifty or sixty good years left in me. You're fifty-one, Mom. You're the one who needs to get laid."

"Rory!" She grabs a pillow off my bed and throws it

at me. "Watch your mouth."

I laugh as I grab a pair of clean skinny jeans and a T-shirt out of the closet then head for the bathroom. My mom watches me curiously, probably waiting for me to tell her why I'm taking a shower right after work instead of right before bed, the way I've done it all my life. Finally, I move to close the bathroom door and she stops it with her hand.

"Do you have a date tonight, young lady?"

I smile at her, knowing she's expecting me to deflect the question. "I may even get laid."

I close the door and shake my head when I hear my mom shout, "Yes!"

TWO HOURS LATER, my mom has left the building and Skippy is sitting at my feet under the dining table, watching me eat a bowl of homemade udon. The folded sheet of paper and Sierra Nevada box are sitting on top of the table in front of me. I clamp my chopsticks around some noodles and bring them to my mouth, slurping the rich broth as I try to decide which one to open first. I know I promised Houston I'd wait for him to open the box for me, but my curiosity is reaching epic levels the longer the box remains unopened. I sigh as I reach for the paper and unfold it, laying it on the table next to my bowl so I can read as I eat.

My dearest Bella,

The love of my life, and I know you didn't want me to mention this but the mother of my child.

I shake my head in dismay. He's going to infuriate his future wife with these vows. If she doesn't want him to mention the pregnancy or the baby, that means she wants to try to hide her baby bump, which is totally her prerogative. At least Benji recognizes he needs help.

I read the rest of the vows to myself, then I read them again aloud, just to see how they sound when spoken. It's even worse. Though Skippy does respond to my recitation by putting his paw on my thigh, so maybe Benji's on to something.

"You want to marry me, Skip?" I say, shaking his paw as he stares at me dumbly.

I finish my udon and clean up, then I plop down on the sofa with Benji's vows. My new best friend, the Sierra Nevada box, keeps watch from the coffee table. I'll attempt to rewrite Benji's vows while I wait for Liam to come over in an hour. The first thing I do is type up what Benji has already written into a notes app on my phone, then I begin thinking about what I would want my future husband to say to me when I get married.

Houston's face materializes in my mind and I

suddenly have trouble breathing. I hold the phone to my chest as I think of him saying the words I've needed to hear for five years. *I was wrong to let you go, and I'd rather die than let it happen again.*

The vibration startles me. I pull the phone away from my chest and I can't believe what I'm seeing. I answer the call and slowly press it to my ear.

"Houston?"

"I'm sorry I couldn't make it to the store today."

The sound of his voice, smooth and sweet with a slight crackly finish, reminds me of toffee. And it makes my chest ache with longing.

"Is everything okay?" I ask, remembering my promise to Troy not to say anything about the things he shared with me today.

Houston is silent for a moment and I count each breath until he responds. "No, actually, everything's pretty messed up right now."

His honesty catches me off my guard. "What are you saying? Are you... Are you getting divorced?"

"I want to, but it's not that simple. I need to see you. Can I come over?"

I let out a deep sigh. "Houston, I can't be on this side of a list of excuses. If you want to be married, you should stay married and stop jerking me around."

"Rory, don't hang up. Listen to me. Just... please listen." He expels a large puff of air, and I brace myself for whatever he's about to say. "My wife is sick.

Mentally, not physically. She's… threatening to kill herself if I leave her. And I know this has nothing to do with you, but you know me. You know… how much I loved Hallie."

Tears well up in my eyes the moment he says her name. "I know," I whisper. "But you can't save everyone, Houston."

I think of how he saved me from having to live in a dorm haunted by my best friend's memory. How he gave me a car to save me from having to drive my shitty Toyota, though I was very lucky I held onto that Toyota or I wouldn't have a car right now. Then, of course, I think of how he saved me from making the mistake of marrying him when he obviously wasn't ready. And how he tried to save Hallie when he found her.

"That's why I want to see you," he replies. "I think… I need you to save me this time."

I bite my lip to keep from turning into a complete sobbing mess. *This* is what I've needed to hear. Not that he was wrong, just that he needs me.

"Rory?"

"Yes?"

"Open your door." His words are followed by a knocking that sends my heart racing.

"Wait. I'll be right there."

I end the call and immediately open my text messaging app. My fingers tremble as I tap out a vaguely honest message to Liam, telling him something came up and I'll have to call him tomorrow. He doesn't respond right away, so I head for the front door. I take a deep breath and let it out as I pull it open.

Houston leans with one hand on my doorframe, a simmering cocktail of quiet desperation and raw sex appeal. His eyes are fixed on mine, communicating silently, but the message is loud and clear as his gaze falls on my lips.

I take a step back. He steps forward. I begin to stumble. His right arm catches me around the waist. His left hand pushes the door closed. The excitement pulsates between us as we stare into each other's eyes.

My gaze wanders over the sharp angles of his cheekbones and jaw. The perfect slope of his nose and the dark desire in his blue eyes. And, *oh*, that mouth. The mouth that spoke the words I couldn't forget. The tongue that taught me how to surrender every part of myself to him.

His fingers brush my cheek. "God, I've missed this," he whispers as he runs his fingers through my hair and tucks it behind my ear.

My arms slacken at my sides as I feel myself dissolving into him with each stroke of his fingers. "What are we doing, Houston?"

He traces his thumb over the shell of my ear, then he gently squeezes my earlobe. My chest heaves as the throbbing between my legs intensifies. His other hand moves up to cup the other side of my face. Cradling my head in his massive hands, he holds my gaze as I grab his wrists to steady myself.

"Whatever you want to do."

He leans forward and I hold my breath. His lips hover over mine. My heart pounds a roaring beat in my ears. I tighten my grip on his wrists. I may collapse at any moment. Then, his mouth is on mine.

His lips are as soft as I remember. His breath hot on my mouth, so hot my insides are burning up. I want to part my lips and kiss him like we haven't seen each other in five years, but I'm afraid. I'm afraid I've never been more afraid.

"I can't," I whisper desperately.

"You can't what?"

"I can't… I can't believe what I'm about to do."

Houston

I THREAD MY fingers through the soft hair at her nape. As I firmly clasp the back of her neck, her head tilts to the side and her lips part for me. The heat of her shallow breaths stir a primal longing inside me. Leaning in closer, I brush my lips over hers and lay a soft kiss on the corner of her mouth. Her lips are still slightly parted as she lets out a soft whimper, waiting for me. Just that small sound is all it takes. My erection grows until it pushes painfully against the zipper of my jeans.

Her willingness to give herself to me is hotter than she could possibly imagine. I kiss her luscious top lip and she exhales as I take it into my mouth and suck gently. Then I tilt my head slightly as my lips cover hers. Our mouths fit together like puzzle pieces, and we let out a collective sigh followed by a soft chuckle.

"I still love you," I murmur into her mouth. "You believe me, don't you?"

She tightens her grip on my forearms. "How could you forget me?"

I tilt my head back to look into her hazel eyes and my stomach twists when I see the tears collecting at the corners. "Forget you? I never forgot you."

"When you first saw me at the store, you didn't recognize me."

I hoped she would have forgotten that embarrassing moment. I consider lying to her and telling her I was only kidding. That I totally recognized her. But if I want any chance of keeping her, I know I have to be honest.

"I started going to a therapist after we broke up, and she treated me for PTSD."

"PTSD? Are you saying I gave you PTSD?"

I chuckle. "No."

"Then what does that have to do with forgetting me?"

She loosens her grip on my arms so I let go of her face and grab her hands.

"I asked her to help me forget what happened with Hallie and she started me on an experimental PTSD treatment that uses anesthesia and CBT to modify painful memories."

"CBT?"

"Cognitive behavioral therapy. They gave me low doses of xenon gas for a few months and I also had to change my behavior whenever something happened that reminded me of the day Hallie died."

"But…"

"Yeah, almost everything associated with you reminded me of Hallie."

She lets go of my arms. "You really forgot me?"

I feel physically sick at this question. Not because I resent the accusation. I resent myself for ever making her feel like I'd forgotten her. As much as I wanted to erase the mistakes I made with Rory and Hallie from my memory, it's impossible to erase the bad stuff without also erasing the good.

"No, you don't understand," I reply, taking both her hands in mine and looking her in the eye. "I went through the program, and it seemed to work for a while, but every day that passed, every visit to my mom's house, and every conversation about Hallie chipped away at what little progress I'd made. The effect wore off. And three years ago, I was pretty much at square one."

She looks up at me and the hurt in her eyes makes me sick with myself. "But you still forgot me because you didn't have any more reminders of me?"

"I could never forget you," I whisper, letting go of one of her hands so I can brush a piece of hair out of her face. "But I tried really hard to because I was in a world of pain after we broke up. And what happened the day we ran into each other two weeks ago was a split-second error. Bad programming. I can prove it to you. Where's the box I gave you?"

Rory

August 24th

THE MOMENT HE lets go of my hands, I'm struck by how cold I feel without his hands on me. Then I remember his question and I turn around to face the coffee table where the Sierra Nevada box sits. I move toward it and Houston follows me, reaching for the box before I can grab it.

"Sit down."

I take a seat on the sofa, but he doesn't follow suit. He stands next to the coffee table, staring at the box in his hands. I wish I knew what he was thinking, because all I can think of right now is the promise I made to him last night. If he shows me what's inside the box, I'm supposed to tell him what my book is about.

Finally, he tears his gaze from the box and tilts his head as he notices the sheet of paper sitting on the coffee table. He's six-foot-four. Can he really read the words scribbled on that worn piece of paper from all the way up there?

"What is that?"

I reach forward and swipe the paper off the table. "It's nothing. It's just something I'm working on for my boss."

"Your boss asked you to help him write his wedding vows?"

Suddenly I feel guilty, as if I've somehow betrayed Houston. "Yes. He found out I have a degree in English and he was kind of desperate for some help. It's not a big deal."

He smiles as he looks down at me. "Can I see what you've written?"

"No!"

He laughs. "Why not?"

"Because I haven't had a chance to write much of anything yet, and it's embarrassing."

"Why is it embarrassing? It's just me." He sits next to me on the sofa and I get a strong whiff of his clean, masculine scent. "Let me see, then I'll open the box."

"I thought you wanted to know what my book is about."

"I want to see both."

His words echo in my mind and the guilt hits me

hard. Houston wants both me and his wife. And I was about to let him have his way.

"You have to leave," I say, tucking the vows into my back pocket as I rise from the sofa.

He stands up with me. "Why? What did I do?"

"It's not what you did. It's—" I'm interrupted by the vibration in my front pocket. I slip my phone out and shake my head when I read the text message.

Liam: *Rory, if you're not ready to go out yet, just let me know. I'd rather keep you as a friend than risk one of us getting hurt.*

"Who's that?" Houston asks, glancing at the back of my phone.

"It's a really nice guy who's not married."

His chest is heaving and his jaw is clenched tightly as the anger percolates inside him. "Don't shut me out, Rory. Give me a chance."

"A chance to do what?"

He doesn't answer right away, so I begin typing a response to Liam. Houston grabs my phone and gently slips it out of my hands. He lays the phone facedown on the coffee table and smiles as he opens the Sierra Nevada box.

I gasp when I see the ring lying on its side. "What is that?"

He lifts my chin up so he can look me in the eye. "I bought this engagement ring for you two weeks before we broke up."

I clutch my chest as I try to keep breathing. "What? I don't understand. You… you said we couldn't get married. You… you broke my heart."

"It was the biggest mistake of my life. I could see it then and I can see it even more now. Letting you go was the single stupidest thing I've ever done." He plucks the ring out of the box and sets the box on the table next to my phone, then he holds the ring between his thumb and forefinger. "Rory, you're the only one who knows me, which is kind of sick because I spent so much of our time together lying to you."

I shake my head in disbelief. "What do you mean?"

He blinks back tears. "There's so many things you don't know about me that I need to tell you, so you'll understand everything that happened back then and afterward." He takes my hand and my entire body trembles, the way it did when I thought he was going to propose to me five years ago. But this time, he lays the ring in the palm of my hand and closes my fingers around it. "This is yours. It's my promise to you. I swear I'm going to do everything I can to get that ring on your finger."

I squeeze my fist around the ring, savoring the sharp prick of the diamond as it digs into my skin. "Houston, I'd rather have the truth than this ring."

"That ring is my promise to tell you the truth, but only when the time is right. I need to get out of my marriage first. I need you to know how serious I am first." He takes my face in his hands again and I draw in a sharp breath. "Promise me you'll wait for me and I promise I'll tell you everything."

I would be stupid to make that kind of deal with a married man, but Houston isn't just any man. He's the only man I've ever loved. He may be the only man I'll ever love. I can't risk throwing it all away again.

"It's about us," I whisper.

He looks confused. "What are you talking about?"

"The book. It's the story of us."

He sighs as if he's been waiting to hear these words all his life. "I hope it never ends." He brushes a tear from my cheek and kisses my forehead. "Wait for me."

I nod and wrap my arms around his waist to bury my face in his chest. He holds me tightly for a long while, occasionally kissing the top of my head and rubbing my back. I breathe in the scent of his warm skin through his T-shirt and I find myself not wanting to let go. Like we could stand here for the rest of our lives and I'd be perfectly content.

A while later, it could be ten minutes or ten days, Houston tilts my face up and the smile on his face makes my heart happy. He leans in to kiss me and I have no desire to stop him anymore. He may not be mine on paper, but I know his heart is mine. I can feel it in the way he kisses me, exactly the way he used to kiss me. Like we've picked up right where we left off, never skipping a beat.

His fingers are tangled in my hair, tugging lightly so my mouth falls open in a silent gasp. Seizing the opportunity, he pushes his tongue farther inside. I close my lips around his tongue and suck gently. His moans drive me crazy. I bob my head a little to give him a preview of what's to come. Then, I release his tongue and smile as I tuck the ring into my pocket.

Reaching up, I coil my arms around his solid neck. His arms lock around my hips as he lifts me up, like I weigh about as much as a sparrow. My legs curl around his waist and I tilt my head back as he kisses my neck.

"I missed you," I whisper.

"I missed the fuck out of you, Scar."

I laugh so hard I almost choke on my saliva. "You killed it."

He carries me over to the sofa and lays me down with the utmost of ease. "What are you talking about? I'm just getting started. Can you feel the love tonight?"

I sigh as he slides his hand under my T-shirt and settles himself between my legs. "I can feel *something*."

His fingers squeeze my breast. "So can I."

He kisses me hard and I lose myself in him until we're a tangled mess of hot, unrestricted desire. Suddenly, his T-shirt and my shirt and bra are off and I don't remember removing them. He's still so good at operating in stealth mode while I'm lost in the throes of lust.

His lips are hot and firm as he kisses his way down to my breast. My back arches the moment he takes my nipple into his mouth. The throbbing between my legs intensifies as he firmly squeezes my other nipple. Tangling my fingers in his hair, I slide my hands down to his shoulders, digging my fingernails into his skin as he devours my sensitive flesh.

"Oh, God, Houston."

"What do you want me to do to you?" he whispers as he kisses his way to my other breast.

Just hearing him ask the question makes me writhe with anticipation, but it's been so long since we've been together, I don't know if I remember how to do this.

He kisses his way down to my navel, his fingers poised on the button of my jeans as he looks up at me with a cunning smile. "I'm going to make you come so hard tonight."

I swallow hard as he undoes my button. "Oh, God."

He slowly eases me out of my jeans, smiling when he sees my pink G-string. Tracing his finger downward along the lacy edge, he stops when his hand is between my legs. He looks up at me, watching my reaction as he slips his finger beneath the fabric and easily finds my clit. My abdominal muscles tighten and I try to focus on breathing as he gently teases me with the soft pad of his finger.

"Look me in the eye."

I gaze back at him, my mouth gaping as he strokes

my clit. He varies the pressure, first soft and then firm, then soft again. I pant steadily, my mewls subdued by my insecurity.

"Let go, baby," he reassures me.

I bite my lip as I look him in the eye and swallow my reserve. My hips buck in time with the rhythm of his hand. And almost instantly, the orgasm hits me in waves. My body curls inward feeding the fiery hunger in his eyes. He holds me tighter, his gaze fixed on mine as my legs twitch with the force of the pleasure. My body spasms uncontrollably as he continues to stroke me, and I get a strong urge to push his hand away. The pleasure is so intense it's almost painful.

"This is mine," he murmurs as he caresses me. "Say it."

I exhale a sharp breath coupled with a moan as the orgasm reaches epic levels. "It's yours."

My thighs tremble and I let out a few sharp whimpers, but he continues until the orgasm passes. He's going for orgasm number two.

"You're going to come so many times tonight, you'll be begging me to stop just so you can catch your breath."

I haven't been touched in so long, the second orgasm comes easily. He smiles as he slides his hand back and slowly pulls my panties off. The moment his mouth is on me, I throw my head back and let out a loud sigh.

"Holy shit."

His tongue swirls around my clit, torturing me, until orgasm number three begins. He senses it, so he pulls his head back and slides two fingers inside me. I look down and he's watching me so he can see when he's found my G-spot. He curls his fingers inside me, massaging in a firm back-and-forth motion until he locates it. My body jumps a little and he smiles as he focuses his stroking on that one sensitive area.

Then his mouth is on me again and the pleasure is almost too much to handle. I grab fistfuls of his hair and try not to kick him as he brings me to orgasm again. He reaches up to tweak my nipple, keeping his mouth closed around my clit. My body quakes violently as he stimulates me beyond the point of comprehension. Until I feel as if I'm panting so hard I'm going to black out.

When he's done, he plants a soft kiss on the inside of my thigh and moves to get up. I watch in wonderment as he stands from the sofa and strips before me. He's more beautiful than I remembered. His perfect pecs and abs flow effortlessly into his oblique muscles, which draw a glorious arrow pointing down toward his velvety smooth erection.

He settles down on top of me and I coil my arms around his muscular shoulders as he kisses me deeply. His erection rubs against my sensitive clit as his hips thrust slowly back and forth, using my moisture to massage me and work me into a frenzy.

I push his shoulders back so I can look him in the eye. "Put it in… please."

The left corner of his mouth curves upward, then we both look down to watch as he slowly slides his cock inside me.

"Fuck," he hisses, as he pushes in a bit farther. "You're so tight." He plunges into me a little at a time, watching my face to see my reaction. "Have you been with anyone else?" He freezes with half his erection inside me when I shake my head. "Really?"

I would expect myself to feel embarrassed about this, but I'm not. I shouldn't be ashamed of the fact that I don't want to have casual sex.

"Is that weird?" I reply.

He smiles and kisses my forehead. "It's not weird. It's sexy as fuck."

He lifts my leg a little so he can slide farther into me. It takes a few minutes, but he finally gets his entire erection inside me and I gasp when he hits my cervix.

His brow furrows as he looks me in the eye. "Am I hurting you?"

I shake my head. "I don't think I've ever been this happy to feel a bit of pain."

He leans down to whisper in my ear. "I love you, Scar."

I tighten my arms and legs around him and close my eyes as I attempt to burn this moment into my memory. "I love you, too."

He pulls his head back a little and grabs my face, forcing me to look him in the eye. "I love you, baby, but tonight I'm going to fuck you until you question that." He smiles and plants a kiss on the tip of my nose as he thrusts his hips back and forth. "I've been waiting five long years for this."

I whimper as he moves in and out of me. His considerable girth gently stretches the walls of my pussy, tenderizing me, preparing me for whatever he has in mind.

I gaze back at him as I whisper, "I'm ready. And I'll never question that."

Houston

Five years ago, January 3rd

"WHAT ARE YOU here for today, young man?"

I swallow hard as I try to work up the courage to say what's on my mind. "My sister died last month and I... I've been having trouble sleeping, and I've... been feeling sort of... sad. Is there something you can give me to make it go away?"

Dr. Greene flashes me a tight smile. "Being sad is not a disease that I can prescribe medication for. Depression is a disease for which I can prescribe an antidepressant, but it is not the same as being sad. Being sad is a single symptom of depression. And depression is not the same thing as grief."

I sigh audibly. "Can't you just give me something to

make it go away?"

"Make *what* go away?"

I want to shout, *The fucking grief!* But my subconscious beats me to it. "The memories."

Dr. Greene casts a pitiful look in my direction and that's when I realize I've diagnosed my own disorder. And I know exactly how to treat it.

I don't need drugs for depression. I need alcohol for forgetting.

I slide off the exam table and grab my coat off the plastic chair. "Sorry I wasted your time. I made a mistake."

By the time I hop into the driver's seat of my truck, I'm shaking like a leaf as the memory of Hallie's death replays in my mind. I told myself I would get over that by getting revenge on the person responsible for her death, but nothing I've done over the past month has brought the justice Hallie deserves. I've only made things even more complicated. I've fallen in love with the person I intended to destroy.

Rory

ALL DAY LONG, no matter what I do or where I go, I can't seem to get rid of the giddy, nerves-zinging sensation. I discussed my thoughts on the wedding vows with Benji and couldn't stop thinking of the engagement ring tucked inside the pocket of my jeans. As Bella taught me how to make a billion different espresso drinks, I grinned stupidly while imagining Houston standing naked in my kitchen, gulping a postcoital glass of water. While passing the produce department on my way out of work, I smiled coyly at the sight of the bananas. So when I step onto the sidewalk outside the store, where Kenny waits to walk me home, he instantly spots me grinning from ear to ear. There will be no hiding from him what happened last night.

Kenny looks me up and down and cocks an eyebrow. "You got your kitten smashed."

I shrug as I fall into step beside him. "Maybe."

"By the lumberjack?"

I chuckle at this. "That's quite a violent image you've conjured, but no. Not the lumberjack."

He grabs my arm and stops me in the middle of the sidewalk on Burnside. "You have *another* suitor I don't know yet? That's not allowed, Aurora."

"Suitor? I didn't realize I needed permission from Sir Kenneth to get my kitten smashed."

"Who is he? Whoever he is better not cut into our quality time."

I smile as I lock arms with him and continue down Burnside. "I can't really say too much about it. He's…" I glance around as if any of the random strangers walking around us are interested in our conversation. "He's married," I whisper just loud enough for Kenny to hear.

"Oh, my goodness," he gasps, covering his mouth. "I didn't know you were such a slut."

I nudge his shoulder. "I'm not a slut. It's complicated. He's my first love. And the only guy I've ever been with."

He shakes his head as if he's trying to physically clear away his confusion. "Whoa, whoa. Wait. So, have you been with this guy the whole time he's been married? I'm so confused… and intrigued."

"No, we broke up five years ago while we were in college. Then he got married and… We ran into each other at the Belmont store."

"While you were working there with me?"

I nod and he gasps.

"Oh, my God, Rory. Was it that guy in the back of the store?"

I nod again and his eyes widen.

"He's gorgeous," he replies, continuing down Burnside. "I am truly jealous."

"You don't think I'm a disgusting human being for having sex with a married man? It was only one night, but I do feel slightly, or maybe totally, ashamed."

He slows down to a stroll and flashes me a warm smile. "Of course not. I know a thing or two about complicated relationships. No one's perfect. And anyone who expects you to be perfect is just hiding something."

I chuckle at this statement. "No one has ever explained that to me so simply. How did you get to be so wise at the age of thirty?"

He gasps and lightly smacks my shoulder. "Don't ever insult me like that again. And my wisdom is just plain common sense earned over a very messed-up childhood. I mean, my mother named me Kenny, for God's sake. You'd be surprised how much crap one person can endure in twenty-two years."

I sigh as I think of how much I had endured by the age of eighteen. "Not surprised at all, actually." I hug his arm. "That was a hug for your messy childhood."

"Thank you. That made it all better."

After Kenny and I gorge ourselves on Korean barbecue tacos at the food truck on Burnside, we head to my place to let our food digest while watching a chick flick. When we arrive at my apartment, I take Skippy out of his crate and walk him outside to do his business. Then I check his blood glucose before I feed him. And he is more than happy to snuggle up with me on the sofa.

Kenny beckons me to cuddle with him while we watch *How to Lose A Guy In 10 Days*. I cock my eyebrow at his invitation, but he waves off my skepticism.

"Oh, come on. You're safe with me. You and I both know cuddling is totally gay."

I scoot closer to him and lay my head on his shoulder. He lies back so he can put his leg on the sofa and I wind up with my head lying on his chest.

He sniffs the top of my head. "Your hair smells delicious. What is that?"

"It's vanilla birthday cake shampoo and espresso. I was making coffee all day."

"It perfect, just like you."

We settle into a comfortable position and soon we're lost in the adorable antics of Kate Hudson and Matthew McConaughey. An hour later, I'm woken by a vibration in my pocket. I glance up and Kenny is still awake and watching the movie. I slide my phone out of my pocket and find a text from Houston.

Houston: *Do you work tomorrow?*

I carefully sit up so I don't poke Kenny with my elbow, then I begin typing my response.

"Is that him?" Kenny asks as he sits up.

"Yes."

"Houston is a cowboy's name. Hmm… A cowboy and a lumbersexual? I'd pay to see that."

I shake my head as I hit send.

Me: *No. I'm taking Skippy to Wallace Park to mingle with his own kind.*

Houston: *How about Wednesday?*

Me: *Yeah, I'll be there.*

Houston: *Good. Bring the ring with you.*

I tuck the phone into my pocket and lean back as I wonder why he wants me to bring the ring to work. When I glance to my left, Kenny's wearing an awkward smile. I'm almost afraid to ask what he's thinking, but I have to know.

"What?"

He shakes his head. "What are you going to do if he

doesn't leave his wife?"

"I don't expect you to understand why I feel this way, but I honestly think that's not something I have to worry about."

"You guys bumped into each other just two weeks ago and you had sex once and now he's just going to leave his wife?"

"We had sex *four* times," I reply with a grin, but Kenny doesn't look impressed. "I told you, it's not that simple. We have a history."

"Enlighten me. What is this *history* that makes the situation so complicated?"

I heave a deep sigh and stare at the ceiling as I begin. "I've loved him since I was eleven years old."

"Holy pedobear. You two were together when you were eleven?"

"No. That's how long I've loved him. We didn't get together until I was eighteen. Houston's sister was my best friend." I close my eyes and take a deep breath as I try to keep my emotions in check. "Hallie committed suicide our freshman year in college and I ended up living with Houston the rest of the year. We broke up a week before summer break."

"So you were there for each other at the most painful time of your lives, but the pain wasn't enough to keep you two together?"

I open my eyes to look at Kenny. "I wish it were that simple." I reach into my pocket and pull out the engagement ring. "He was really messed up by what happened to Hallie. He was the one who found her."

"Holy jeebus. Look at the size of that rock. He gave you this engagement ring and you *still* broke up with him?"

"No. He gave me that ring last night. He never gave it to me when we were together. He broke up with me when he found out I was pregnant."

Kenny shakes his head adamantly as he rises from the sofa. "Uh-uh, Rory. This isn't *complicated*. This is Kardashian-level *fucked up*. You're gonna need to get me a stiff drink if you expect me to listen to this."

I laugh as I get up and head for the kitchen to get some tequila and lime wedges. I rarely ever drink, hence the easy buzz I got when Kenny and I went out last weekend. I think drinking is one of the things that reminded me too much of Houston. The tasting parties and the research trips to the pubs. Getting tipsy and having frenzied drunken sex was so common for us that just walking down the beer aisle at work can be a haunting experience.

Two hours and four tequila shots later, Kenny has heard the story of Houston and me. I've arrived at the climax where, apparently, Houston comes back into my life, gives me a very expensive diamond engagement ring, and tells me he's going to leave his wife. And it all happens at the same time I run into a totally nice, unattached lumberjack I once knew in a past life.

"Oh, I almost forgot!" I pull my phone out of my pocket and Kenny lunges for it, but I hold it out of his reach. "I told lumberjack—I mean, Liam—I'd call him today. I have to call him."

"Nuh-uh. You are not drunk-dialing him at eleven o'clock at night on a Monday. Give me that phone."

I laugh as he struggles to take the phone from me, then I jump up from the sofa and race to the bedroom, laughing maniacally as I lock the door behind me.

"Nothing good can come of this!" he shouts at me through the door.

I dial Liam's number, then I press my fingertips to my cheekbones to see how numb my face is. He answers on the second ring.

"Hey."

"Hey," I reply, trying not to laugh.

"I thought you'd forgotten about me."

"Nope. Just got a little sidetracked. I'm drunk."

He laughs. "You drunk-dialed me?"

"Yeah, sorry. I was drinking with my friend and I just remembered that I promised to call you today. I didn't want you to think I'm flaky. I'm really not flaky, but I am forgetful. And both of those words begin with the letter *F*."

He chuckles. "An astute observation. Other than getting drunk, what are you and your friend doing?"

"Exchanging sob stories." I hear a soft barking noise in the background and I get really excited. "Do you have a dog?"

"Yeah, a shepherd mix named Sparky, short for Sparkle Motion."

I chuckle at this reference to the movie *Donnie Darko*. "He must be a great dancer."

"He is. You should see him go from a pirouette straight into a perfect *Dirty Dancing* lift."

"I'd love to see that. Maybe he could teach Skippy a thing or two. I'm taking Skip to Wallace Park tomorrow. You should bring Sparky."

Liam is silent for a moment, and when he finally responds his voice sounds a bit weary. "Rory, tomorrow's Tuesday. I work tomorrow."

"Oh, crap. Sorry. Sometimes I forget that not everyone works retail. Just forget I asked. I'll let you go. You probably need to get to sleep so you can wake up early. Sorry."

"Wait. Don't hang up. I'm just... Ah, fuck it. I'll meet you at the park tomorrow at ten a.m. But you're really drunk right now, so I'm calling you at nine a.m. to remind you, 'kay?"

Suddenly I feel a little sick to my stomach as I realize Liam is going to skip work tomorrow to hang out with me. I want to tell him to just forget it. I don't want to lead him on. But Liam was the one who said he'd rather be friends with me than risk getting hurt. I guess that means I'll have to come clean with him tomorrow about Houston.

"Okay. See you tomorrow."

I open the door and Kenny is wearing a look of disappointment. "You just asked him on a date."

"No, I didn't," I reply, making my way to the kitchen to rehydrate with a glass of water. "I asked him if he wanted to meet me at the dog park. That's not a date."

"Don't play coy with me, young lady. You can't pass this off as a doggy playdate. That lumberjack thinks you're interested in more than his dog."

My buzz is wearing off quickly as I reach for a glass in the cupboard. "Even if that's true, the point of this date is to clarify that. I can do it over the phone, but he's the one who said he wanted to be friends with me."

Kenny sighs as he leans against the counter. "Fine. But if you break his heart, make sure you do enough damage that he turns gay."

I laugh as I fill my glass with water from the tap. "Now you're into lumbersexuals?"

"Honey, a luxurious beard works wonders for oral sex."

"Ew!"

"Don't knock it till you try it!"

Houston

August 26th

THE SMILE ON Troy's face tells me he's very pleased with my plans. "You're finally gonna do it?"

I take a long pull on my bottle of Barley Legal Double IPA. "I know. It's been a long time coming, but I'm still nervous as fuck."

Steve, the bartender in the Barley Legal pub, exchanges my empty bottle for a fresh, cold one. I nod at him and he goes back to pouring some pints for a group of girls who came in on one of those Portland brewery bike tours. Not that I don't appreciate the extra business, but riding around on a bike while drinking beer all day sounds like a good way to get hit by a bus.

"So when are you gonna do it? Can I get it on

video?"

I shake my head. "Tessa's gonna flip. It might be a good idea for someone to be outside in case she pulls out a gun or something. I don't know what the fuck she's been doing behind my back, but I could totally see her at the gun range aiming at a poster of me."

"Dude, she's crazier than a coked-up raccoon. You'd better watch yourself."

"I can handle Tessa. And she's not crazy, she's sick."

"Whatever." He takes a few gulps from his glass of double bock. "You didn't ask me what happened when I ran into Rory the other day."

"I assumed you were probably scheming to sway her in my direction. I didn't send you there by mistake."

"You fucking bastard."

I shrug as I bring the bottle to my lips. "I need all the help I can get."

"That's what friends are for," he replies.

"Interesting. When I was with your mom last night, she said friends are for cock-gobbling."

Troy strokes his chin as if he's considering this. "That *is* interesting because *your* mom said friends are for enemas. Followed by sweet backdoor action, of course."

"Of course." I leave half my beer in the bottle and slide off the bar stool. "I'll see you tomorrow, brother."

"Good luck, man."

It's eleven a.m. when I leave the pub. As I open the door to get into the SUV, I spot a silver Lexus that looks like Tessa's parked at the end of the block. I can't be sure, but it doesn't look like there's anyone sitting in the driver's seat. I shake my head as I hop into my car. There must be dozens of silver Lexuses in this area at any given time. I'm being paranoid.

I've only had one and a half beers, so I decide to drive by Wallace Park to see if Rory is still there with her dog. Seeing her will give me the motivation I need to break away from Tessa.

Being with Rory two nights ago was like being myself again after five years of pretending to be someone else. I finally felt like I was living more than half a life. The worst part is that I didn't even realize I was living in black and white until I bumped into Rory two weeks ago. Now I can't get the color of her hair and the taste of her skin out of my head.

I want to carve out a place for her in my life, sow the seeds of trust, and watch our story grow. I want to stir up the ideas in her mind and drink in the tales she'll tell me into the early hours of the morning.

I want to bore into her, physically and mentally, unearthing every glistening jewel of pleasure and pain. I want to take her to bed every night and worship at the altar of her hushed beauty. I want to lose myself in the luscious curves of her hips and the delicate scent of her skin.

I want to slide that ring on her finger and kiss her madly in front of hundreds of people. I want to have a family with her. I want to make her deliriously happy.

I turn left on Raleigh Street and quickly find a space for my car across from the park on the corner of Raleigh and 25th. I cross the street, trying to peek through the trees and the wire mesh fence surrounding the dog park, but I don't see anyone. I head through the waist-high gate and I finally glimpse some people and dogs in the grassy open field. I spot the black Labrador first, which has to be Rory's dog, Skippy. He's playing with a tan dog that appears to be some kind of shepherd mix. My gaze follows the dogs as they run, tongues wagging, toward an area shaded by some trees.

I'm about twenty yards from the trees when the black Lab collides with Rory. She orders the dog to sit, but I quickly lose sight of what she's doing when I notice the guy standing next to her. It's the guy who went to her apartment the other night.

A roaring wave of jealousy swells inside me, flooding my veins with pure adrenaline. My fists are urging me to destroy him, the one thing standing between Rory and me and everything we've ever wanted. But my brain is yelling at me, *Down, boy. Sit. Stay.*

I approach slowly, consciously trying not to clench my fists so I don't look *too* intimidating. Rory spots me when I'm a few yards away. Her eyes widen and she drops the dog treat in her hand, which the tan dog quickly snatches up.

"Houston?" she says, her voice breathy with shock.

She glances at the guy next to her and he refuses to look at me, but the sight of the muscle in his jaw twitching drives me over the edge. This asshole thinks *I'm* inconveniencing *him*? He's the one infringing on *my* territory.

"Is there a problem?" I ask, my voice taut with tension.

Rory opens her mouth to respond when she realizes I'm not talking to her. "No!" she shouts, as if we're two dogs who can be called off each other with a simple command. "No, this is not happening here, or anywhere, so just come off it."

I tear my gaze away from the hipster lumberjack and look Rory in the eye. "We need to talk."

I nod for her to follow me and she calls Skippy to join us as we walk a few yards away. "Houston, this is not what you think it is. Liam is just a friend."

"It doesn't matter what you think it is. What matters is what *he* thinks it is. And he doesn't think you two are just friends."

"You're misreading this. Really."

I gaze into her hazel eyes, searching for a trace of deceit, but Rory has always been the most honest person I know. She really thinks they're just friends.

"I'm leaving Tessa tonight."

She draws in a sharp breath. "Tonight?"

"Yeah. I need to know if you're ready to do this. Just you and me. See where the story takes us."

She smiles and nods as her eyes well up with tears. "I'm ready."

I cradle her face in my hands and kiss her forehead. "I'll tell you everything tomorrow." I kiss her cheekbone and she grabs the front of my shirt. "Then I hope you'll let me put that ring on your finger."

She exhales a soft sigh into my mouth as I kiss her slowly. I let go of her face and smile when I see the far-off look in her eyes.

"How do you do that?" she murmurs.

I crouch down and scratch Skippy behind the ears as he licks my face. "Do what?"

"Make me forget where I am."

I smile as I look up at her. "That's because everywhere we're together is the only place and the only moment that exists."

Rory

HOUSTON LAUGHS AS Skippy shoves his head into his lap, begging for even more attention. I shake my head as I watch my boy hamming it up, then I glance over my shoulder at Liam. He has Sparky by the collar as the dog jumps up and down excitedly, eager to join his new buddy Skippy. I want to invite Liam and Sparky to come over, but I feel like it would be too awkward. And I don't want to give Houston the wrong impression about Liam and me.

"Houston, I know you've already met Liam, but can I please reintroduce you?"

He takes a deep breath before he stands up, glances in Liam's direction, then flashes me a reluctant smile.

"Anything you want."

"Thank you."

I tear my gaze away from his gorgeous face and turn back to Liam. I wave at him, but he doesn't notice me. I take a step toward him and suddenly I'm knocked onto the grass face-first.

"Tessa! What the fuck?" Houston roars.

It takes me a moment to realize I've been hit in the head with something. I reach up to feel the back of my head, but I'm yanked backward by my hair. The whiplash cracks the joint in my neck, then it's over as quickly as it began and I'm lying facedown on the grass again.

"What the fuck are you doing?" Houston's voice sounds panicked, but I can barely hear it over the sound of Skippy and Sparky's barking.

"Is that her?" a shrill female voice echoes inside my skull. "I knew you were cheating on me!"

"Rory, are you okay?"

I turn my head toward Liam's voice and Skippy's tongue sloshes across my nose several times. "I think so."

"It's over, Tessa. Let it go."

Houston's words make my chest ache as Liam helps me sit up. I can't help but be reminded of the time Houston whispered those same words in my ear. If anyone knows how this woman feels right now, it's me. If she didn't knock me over the head, I might actually empathize with her.

When I'm sitting up, I finally see her. Her blonde shoulder-length hair is as wild as the look in her eyes. She's breathing heavily, seething with anger as she brandishes a steel thermos in her right hand. I rub the back of my head, wincing at the sharp pain.

Houston is standing like a six-foot-four wall of muscle between me and his wife. He looks back at me over his shoulder, a worried expression in his blue eyes. I gasp loudly when his wife takes a swipe at him with the thermos.

"Watch out!" I scream.

She hits Houston square in the side of his head and he curses as he covers his ear.

"Call 911," I urge Liam, but he's already on it.

"Let it go, Tessa," Houston repeats the phrase, and I finally understand he's referring to the thermos, not the marriage.

I'm sure he could easily take it away from her, but he probably doesn't want to be seen in public struggling with a woman. That could easily be misconstrued if a stranger were to stumble upon the scene.

She throws the thermos at Houston's face and he catches it in his right hand. "It's all your fault. Everything is your fault!" she shrieks. "I hope you're happy knowing you killed your baby."

She takes off running toward the street and Houston drops the thermos onto the grass as he takes off after her. My heart is pounding so hard, my fingers are going numb. I grab Skippy and pull him into my lap so he doesn't chase after them. And so I can hug him.

"Should I go after them?" Liam asks, holding his phone to his ear in one hand, his other hand clenched around Sparky's collar so he doesn't bolt after Houston and Tessa.

I nod as I stand up so I can grab on to both Sparky and Skippy. Liam takes off in the same direction as Houston and Tessa, his phone still pressed to his ear. But seconds later, everything seems to stop. Sound. Time. My heart. Everything.

The sound of tires squealing is followed by a loud crash.

"*NO!*" Houston roars so loudly, his cry ruptures the silence.

Liam picks up his pace toward Raleigh Street and I let the dogs pull me after him, though I almost don't want to know what we'll find. I think I'm going to be sick. But I keep putting one foot in front of the other until we're at the fence surrounding the dog park. I take the dogs through the gate and they whimper as they try to pull away from me. Their instincts kick in as they sense someone needs their help.

A leaf falls off a large elm tree and flutters across my line of sight. Only then do I realize I'm crying. I move forward slowly toward the space between my Toyota and Liam's truck. The first thing I see is an Asian woman standing on the sidewalk across the street. She's covering her mouth and staring wide-eyed at something on the other side of the truck. Skippy, Sparky, and I squeeze through the gap between the vehicles and the scene is laid out before me.

Tessa is lying facedown on the asphalt and Houston is on his knees next to her. Liam is standing over them, his phone still pressed against his ear as he looks up and down the street. Probably looking for any sign of an emergency vehicle. My heart stutters when I see Tessa's arm move. She attempts to roll onto her back, but Houston stops her.

"Don't move, baby. The ambulance is on the way."

The word *baby* coming out of Houston's mouth in reference to another woman makes me sick to my stomach. And when I think about the fact that the other woman is his wife, this only makes me sicker. I have no right to be sickened. *I'm* the other woman.

Liam spots me standing between his truck and my car and shakes his head. I don't know what he means by this, but I take it to mean that I don't need to watch. They have it covered.

I turn around and lead the dogs back onto the sidewalk. I unlock my car and let them into the backseat. Then I sink down onto the curb, rest my head in my hands, and cry as I replay the events of the past twenty-four hours over and over in my mind.

Oh, God. What have we done?

It seems that without knowing it, we fell into the

same pattern we fell into five years ago. We were so busy looking in the rearview mirror, we didn't realize we were about to crash. Only this time, it wasn't just Houston and me who got hurt.

Houston

Five years ago, December 4th

HALLIE RARELY CALLS me during the week. She almost always saves her calls to me for the weekend. Then she'll blabber on and on about her classes or all her suggestions for the many ways I should ask Rory on a date. I should never have expressed interest in Rory last Christmas Eve. It was a huge mistake. Rory was still seventeen and I was twenty. I knew she was off limits. But that tight white sweater dress she wore to Christmas Eve dinner at our house completely changed the way I saw her. Then, when I saw her laughing as she and Hallie shook the presents to try to guess what was inside, laughing about vibrators as Christmas gifts, it was like a switch was flipped inside me. And I wasn't able to stop thinking about her for months.

Then I started going out with Kim a couple of months ago, a few months after Rory turned eighteen, and Kim's been doing an okay job of keeping my mind off my sister's friend. But that hasn't stopped Hallie from trying to set us up. She insists Rory and I belong together, whatever the fuck that means. I think it's possible to believe you belong with *anyone* if you spend enough time with them. It's like Stockholm syndrome.

Nevertheless, I'm surprised to see Hallie's name flashing on my phone screen on a Thursday morning. If it were anyone else, I'd hit the red ignore button. But part of being a big brother to a pretty girl like Hallie is that I always worry about her when she's not around. Especially now that she's in college.

I hit the green button to answer the call and whisper into the phone so my Financial Markets professor can't hear. "Hey."

"Houston, I need you to come over here at one o'clock."

"Why?"

"I need to talk to you… about Rory… before she gets back from class. Please." Hallie's voice sounds strangled as if she's been crying or she's about to start.

"Are you okay?"

She lets out a frustrated sigh. "Yes. Will you come?"

"Yeah, I'll be there."

"At one o'clock. Don't forget. And don't be late.

Rory gets here at two so you need to come before that. Okay?"

Professor Hardwick casts a sharp glare in my direction.

"Yeah, yeah. I'll be there."

I end the call and flash the professor a tight smile as I tuck my phone back into my pocket. I don't know what Hallie needs to talk about, but it better be more urgent than another attempt to set me up with Rory. If it's not, I'll need to have a stern discussion with her about calling me during class.

An hour and forty minutes later, I pull my hood over my head and trudge through the light snow across campus to Hamilton Complex. The snow showed up as soon as we got back from Thanksgiving break three days ago. Most everyone grumbles about it, but we hardly ever got snow in McMinnville so I've enjoyed it since coming to UO three years ago.

The snow crunches under my boots and the fresh white powder reminds me of Rory in that dress. I wonder what Hallie wants to talk to me about. Maybe she's going to tell me that Rory's really a man and I can stop lusting after her. Or maybe she's not even going to be in the dorm when I get there. Maybe she's tricked me and Rory into meeting up without her. The same way she used to force her Barbie and Ken dolls to go on dates. *Now kiss!*

I enter Watson Hall at Hamilton Complex and make

my way up to the third floor corridor. I reach room 301, Hallie and Rory's dorm room, and knock three times. Hallie doesn't answer so I knock a little harder this time, in case she's wearing her headphones. That's when I notice the door isn't closed all the way. I knock again, in case she's changing or something, then I push the door in slowly.

"I'm coming in," I say, announcing myself as an extra precaution.

Once the door is all the way open, my vision blurs. My heart gets a massive jolt, like a horse kick in the chest. Hallie is lying in her twin bed, a clear plastic bag over her head. I rush in and quickly undo the Velcro around her neck. I yank off the bag, but she doesn't open her eyes.

"Hallie, this isn't funny. Wake up!" I shake her shoulders. I yell her name. But she doesn't respond. "What the fuck?"

I glance at the bag on the floor and notice a couple of plastic tubes that must have fallen out when I tore the bag off. The tubes lead to a helium tank. *What the fuck was she doing?*

"Wake up, Hal!" I shout, crouched at her bedside as I press two fingers to her neck to check for a pulse. "Come on. This can't be happening. This can't be fucking happening. No, no, no. What were you thinking?"

I can't find a pulse. I stand up and pull my phone out

of my pocket to dial 911, but I'm interrupted when I notice a white envelope clutched in Hallie's right hand. My heart hurts so much, I'm afraid I might be having a heart attack. I reach for the envelope and let out a wretched groan when her stiff fingers don't immediately let go.

I cover my mouth to stifle the sobs when I see my name written on the envelope. She planned this. From the moment she called me two hours ago, and probably well before that, she knew.

"Hey, what's going on here?"

I whip my head around at the sound of the female voice and for a moment I'm terrified it's Rory. But when I turn around it's a brunette I don't recognize.

"Call 911!" I shout at her. "Now!"

"Holy shit," she whispers as she fumbles in her pocket for her phone.

I learned CPR when I was sixteen and I got a summer job as a lifeguard, but I never expected I would need to use what I learned to try to bring my baby sister back from the dead. I scoop her up off the bed and lay her gently on the floor. Then I proceed with the chest compressions and mouth-to-mouth.

My mind knows it's too late, but my heart tells me to keep going. So I keep plunging her fragile breastbone and pumping breath after breath into her deflated lungs. When the paramedics arrive, it takes them a moment to pry my arms from around her limp body. Then, I begin to lose time.

I see flashes of what's happening around me, but I can't make sense of any of it. It's as if my body is here, tucked in the corner of Hallie's dorm, watching as the medics work on her, but my mind is somewhere else. This must not be happening. Or it's happening to someone else. That's not my sister. That is *not* my sister.

I collapse onto the wooden desk chair in the corner of the dorm and it's as if the hardness of the chair has woken me to the harsh reality I've found myself trapped in. Hallie is placed on a stretcher and the medic continues to apply chest compressions as they roll her out of the dorm.

What time is it? If Rory gets here now, she'll be beyond shattered. I reach into my pocket to check the time on my phone as I follow the stretcher down the corridor. It's 1:36 p.m. Hallie said Rory would be here at two. She obviously didn't want Rory to find her, either. But why did she want me to find her? Did she think I could handle this better than Rory?

They wheel the stretcher into the elevator and I squeeze inside with them, trying not to look at her gray skin.

The medic who's pumping the oxygen bag sees my discomfort and offers me his condolences. "I'm sorry, man."

"Why do you guys keep doing that? She's obviously dead."

"Do you have a DNR for her?" the guy applying the chest compressions asks. "If not, we have to keep doing this until she gets to the hospital."

It's a cold response. No apology or attempt at consolation. Just a big *Shut the fuck up and let us do our job.* I want to shove him into the wall of the elevator, maybe break his head open, so he'll stop repeatedly crushing my dead sister's chest. This day couldn't possibly get any worse, could it?

It can. I need to honor Hallie's final words to me and make sure Rory doesn't make it back to the dorm before I explain everything to her. I can't let her come back from class and find out on her own from some stranger.

When the elevator reaches the first floor, I let the medics out first. I follow behind them a few more paces, ignoring the onlookers, then I poke the oxygen bag operator on his shoulder.

"Do you need me to ride with you or can I meet you all at the hospital? I have to call my family."

"No, go ahead and do what you need to do. She's going to Sacred Heart on Hilyard."

I call my mom as I head back to the dorm, but I can't understand a word she says after I break the news to her. Her incoherent wailing fills my chest with an excruciating ache. Somehow, I maintain enough composure to convince her to call a friend so she can get a ride to the hospital.

When I get to the third floor, the campus police have

blocked off the entrance to Hallie's dorm to conduct their investigation. I keep glancing at the time on my phone as I answer their questions. Finally, one of the officers asks me why I keep looking at my phone.

I squint at him in disbelief. "You have some fucking nerve to ask me that. My sister just committed suicide. I promised my mom I'd call her back after I talked to you all. And I have to notify the people that care about her before they find out from someone else. Are we done here?"

He looks like he's ready to chew me out, but his partner beats him to it. "We're good. If we need anything else, we'll give you a call," he says, patting my arm. "Sorry about your sister."

"Yeah, thanks."

I turn to head back toward the elevator when I see Rory stepping out into the corridor. Her eyes are wide with fright and her fair skin is flushed pink. Someone must have already told her what happened.

"No!" she wails as she sees the officers and the crime scene tape over the door. "Hallie!" She races toward us and I catch her around the waist to stop her. "Where is she?"

"She's gone." My voice is gruff and shaky as the tears return. "Hallie's gone."

"No! Stop lying! Let me go!"

She fights me every step of the way as I carry her back to the elevator. Once we're in the cabin, she stops fighting and collapses into a heap on the floor. When the elevator reaches the first floor, I help her up and we both walk out of Hamilton Complex in a daze.

I have to call my mom to make sure she found a ride, but I can't bring myself to do it with Rory here. I know it will only cause her to break down. Ten minutes later, Rory and I arrive at the Jordan Schnitzer Museum of Art. Instinctively, I grab her hand and lead her up the icy steps toward the entrance. We need to get out of the cold, though I'm not sure it matters. I don't think either of us can feel anything right now.

I fumble in my wallet when they ask for my student ID so they can let us in for free. We walk the halls like zombies, searching for something to bring us back to life, some piece of art that proves beauty transcends pain, but nothing stands out. We reach the Reflection Garden and head outside again, undaunted by the dusting of snow covering the path around the reflection pool.

The garden is small and empty, so we instantly gravitate toward the stone statues. Two genderless stone figures kneel in front of a large stone shell. One figure plays a flute while the other strums a small instrument held against its chest. We stare at the statues for a moment before Rory finally speaks.

"I can't go back there."

Fat tears roll down her cheeks and I glance over my shoulder, hoping no one comes out here to interrupt us. Then I take her in my arms and she sobs into my chest, thick, pitiful cries that sound about as pleasing as nails on a chalkboard. But only because I can't make them stop.

"You don't have to go back. You can stay with me."

She sniffs loudly and draws in a stuttered breath. "No, I can't."

She lets go of me and covers her face. I reach up and gently pry her hands away, but she still won't look at me. Her eyelids are puffy and the whites of her eyes are bloodshot, but she looks even more beautiful than she did when I first noticed her in that white dress.

"Yes, you can. You're coming to my apartment now."

"I can't. I need my stuff."

"We'll get it later. Besides, I have to go somewhere private so I can call my mom." I brush the moisture away from her cheek. "Come with me. I don't think I can do it alone."

She finally looks up at me, but she only meets my gaze for a second before she turns away. "Okay." She tucks her hands into her coat pockets and stares at the statues for a moment. "She told me not to come back until two. Why were you already there?"

"She told me to come at one. She said you were coming back at two."

She shakes her head and wipes more tears. "My class ended at 12:30. She texted me and told me not to come back till two. I just don't understand why."

I think of the white envelope tucked in my back

pocket, and consider opening it up right here, but it was addressed to me, not Rory. I have to open it alone.

I place my hand on the small of her back and lead her back into the museum. "We may never know why."

Houston

August 27th

THE WALK UP to Rory's apartment feels like a death march. I couldn't call her to let her know I was coming. I didn't know if she'd actually see me. And I'm sick at the thought that Liam may be in there with her. After what happened yesterday, I have no right to question who Rory spends time with. And after what I'm about to do today, I have no doubt that I'll probably never be with Rory again.

I knock on the door and try not to look at the peephole. I can hear the jingling from the tags on Skippy's collar. I stare at the doorknob, waiting for it to move, but nothing happens.

I step forward and lean my face closer to the

doorframe. "Rory, please open the door."

Skippy lets out a soft bark followed by a desperate whine. I hear her shushing him, but he responds with another baleful howl. The doorknob begins to turn and I step back so I don't startle her. Skippy wags his tail and whimpers as I greet him with a good scratching around his scruff.

"Skippy, get inside."

Rory issues this order a few times before he listens to her. She turns to me and fixes me with a dark glare replete with five years of resentment. After a moment, she steps aside and waves me in.

"I know I'm probably the last person you want to see right now."

"I had to call the hospital myself to try to find out if she was alive and, of course, they wouldn't tell me anything. Yeah, you could have at least texted me."

"She's fine. It's just a broken arm. How's your head?"

"*Now* you care?" She scowls at me for a moment, letting her disdain sink in before she snatches the Sierra Nevada box off the coffee table and holds it out to me. "I don't want this."

I clench my jaw against the wave of nausea that sweeps through me as I take the box from her. "She wasn't pregnant. She was *never* pregnant. She was lying."

"Thanks for clearing that up."

I heave a deep sigh and let it out slowly as I look her

in the eye. "Rory, I came here because I told you I would tell you the truth and I intend to keep my word."

"The truth about *what*?" she demands. "It's over Houston. There is no truth that needs to be spoken anymore."

I shake my head. "I wish that were true." She watches intently as I reach into my back pocket and retrieve the white envelope containing Hallie's suicide letter. "She left a note."

She stares at me for a moment, her face contorted in a mixture of horror and confusion.

"Not Tessa. Hallie."

The confusion quickly morphs to a fury I've never seen, then she pushes me square in the chest. "I hate you!"

"I didn't want you to read it until you were strong enough."

Skippy barks as Rory tries to pummel my chest. I tilt my head back, out of her reach, then I drop the letter so I can grab her wrists.

"That's not for you to decide!" she says, the anguish choking her words. "How could you keep that from me?"

"I was just trying to protect you."

She groans so loudly it sounds like a thunderous roar. "I wish you would stop protecting me! If it weren't for your stupid protection, I wouldn't be picking up the pieces of my life again."

I grit my teeth at the truth in her words. "I need you to read it while I'm here. I… I won't leave until you've read the whole thing. Then you'll understand why."

She yanks her wrists out of my grasp and gently pushes Skippy out of the way so she can snatch the letter off the floor. She heads to the sofa and the dog hops onto the cushion next to her. I sit on the coffee table, facing her so I can see her reaction when she reads the letter. I know the moment she opens that envelope, everything is going to hell. And even if she claims to hate me and resents my attempts to protect her, she's going to need someone to hold, or someone to punch, when she's done reading Hallie's words.

Her hands tremble violently as she stares at my name scrawled on the outside of the envelope. Judging by the tears rolling down her cheeks, she recognizes the handwriting. I hold my breath as I watch her slip the folded five-page letter out of the envelope. She unfolds it slowly and covers her mouth the moment she sees it's genuine. Clutching the letter to her chest, she closes her eyes as she takes a few deep breaths. Finally, she holds it up and begins reading the words that changed my life forever. The words that gave me a purpose and a love like no other while also destroying everything I knew to be true.

Dear Houston,

First of all, please don't show this letter to anyone else. Not Mom. Not Dad. And especially not Rory. And please forgive me for what I've done, and what I'm about to do.

You're probably wondering why I did this. You think there weren't any signs and that none of it makes sense. You think I had everything going for me and so much to live for. But you need to know the truth. And the short version of the truth is that I was destroyed by love. Now let me give you the long version.

It all began about twenty-eight months ago. I was sixteen and it was the end of the summer before my junior year. Rory and I had made plans to go to the movies on a Friday night, but when I got to her house an hour early, she wasn't there yet. No one answered the door. So I went down the driveway toward the backyard to see if she was laying out trying to catch a suntan, but she wasn't there. But her dad was back there, standing on a tall ladder and cutting branches off the big elm tree in their backyard.

He didn't have a shirt on. His T-shirt was draped over one of the lower branches. The tanned skin of his back was glistening with sweat. He'd been working on getting the yard ready for the fall for a couple of weekends. But it wasn't until that day, when I was able to look at him without wondering if Rory was watching me, that I finally realized what a beautiful body he had.

I'd always thought James was handsome. Even as a young girl, I thought he was the coolest dad ever. When I first met Rory and she told me her dad used to be an activist and now he was a lawyer, I thought there probably wasn't anyone in our town as cool as him. But I didn't really develop a crush on him until I found him sawing the branches off that tree.

It wasn't just the sight of the muscles working under his skin, it was the thought of what they were working for. He was working to make the yard better for his family. Rory's mom hated it when the elm tree dumped all its leaves in the fall and winter. And Rory hated it when she had to spend the weekend raking leaves, so he was trying to make their life easier by trimming the tree before autumn.

I think I was feeling more vulnerable that day because I hadn't seen Dad in almost five months, since I visited him in Salem during Spring Break. But he kept making excuses for why we shouldn't visit him that summer, so we gave up trying by the end of June. If I had not been feeling so vulnerable, maybe none of this would have happened. I don't know.

All I know is that it took a few minutes for James to realize I was watching him. He was friendly as he explained that Rory and her mom had to go to the store to pick up a few things for a teachers' potluck at school. He said I could wait inside the house, but I told him it was a nice day so I'd just wait on the back deck. The truth was that I just wanted to watch him.

He didn't seem to catch on the first three or four times I showed up when I knew Rory and her mom would be gone. I told him a couple of times that I had accidentally changed the time on my phone when I reset my alarm clock, which was why I kept showing up at the wrong times, and he seemed to believe me. But *when I showed up at their house a couple of days before the first day of school, he finally caught on.*

It was about seven o'clock at night and Rory and her mom had left to go shopping for school clothes. When James answered the door, he didn't bother telling me that Rory was gone or that she'd be back in a couple of hours. He didn't even invite me in, he just flashed me a reserved smile and opened the door.

I was so nervous. I had been up late the night before trying to figure out how I was going to approach him. School would be starting soon and I thought my opportunities to be alone with him would dry up. I knew I was crazy, but I didn't care. I couldn't stop thinking about him and, in my mind, something had to be done or things would get very awkward very quickly.

I wore a short, flouncy skirt and the UO T-shirt you'd bought for me. I thought this would lull him into a sense of false security, like I wasn't actually sixteen.

He sat down on one end of the sofa and kept on watching Monday night football while I sat on the other end and pretended to wait for Rory. It took a few minutes for me to work up the courage to slip out of my flip-flops and put my feet up on the coffee table the way Rory and I normally did when we were hanging out in her living room. I watched him from the corner of my eye as I crossed and uncrossed my legs. He seemed to be stealing glances every few minutes, so I upped my game by scratching a pretend itch on the inside of my knee, then I left my hand resting between my legs. This got his attention.

He stared at my hand for a moment before he looked up at me and said, "That's a nice skirt."

I was so desperate for more praise, I could hardly speak or breathe. But no matter what position I sat in or how many times I scratched an itch, he never said another word to me that night. Over the next twenty-two months, things went on the same way. Occasionally, I'd find myself alone with him and, occasionally, he would compliment me, but he never touched me or made any verbal propositions. Still, I knew he was interested. And I had convinced myself that everything would change when I turned eighteen. And it did.

Rory and I drove to Salem for my eighteenth birthday. We actually went on May 17th, three days after my birthday, because we had to wait until the weekend. We snuck a bottle of Mom's whiskey out there and got drunk before we went to the Enchanted Forest theme park. It was the best birthday ever. Once we were sober, we drove back to Rory's and got ready for bed.

About one in the morning, I got out of bed to go to the restroom when I saw a faint glow coming from the staircase. I decided to creep downstairs and see if it was James, and it was. He was in the downstairs office with his computer on. I tiptoed in, but he looked up from his laptop immediately. His eyes scanned my body for a few seconds before he told me to close the door.

I closed the door and locked it just to be safe, then I slowly walked around the desk. I was a little disappointed when I saw him working on a legal brief instead of watching porn. But the disappointment melted away when he beckoned me to sit on his lap.

He spoke to me softly, asking how my birthday went and how I felt about going away to UO after the summer. With my head resting on his shoulder, he stroked my leg with the tips of his fingers as he spoke. He told me about the case he was working on and it made me feel smart. But I knew if I didn't make a move, he would probably send me upstairs unsatisfied.

The scent of his skin was crisp and cool like he had just showered, so I took a chance and kissed his neck. He froze and I began to wonder if I had misread his kindness. Maybe he was just comforting me, indulging my schoolgirl crush on my birthday. But then I felt something going on beneath me and I knew he was getting excited.

He told me multiple times that this would only happen once. That he was only doing this because he knew how much I wanted him. And that it could never happen again. But I didn't care.

Part of me believed it would be the last time, but a larger part of me knew I could make it happen again. And I did.

Why do you think I got a summer job thirty-five minutes away from home? James and I would meet at a hotel where he would pay cash, but I put my debit card on file and used my name to register. I was crazy with jealousy when I wasn't with him and I was miserable with guilt every time we parted. I knew I couldn't ask him to leave his wife, so we just never spoke of those kinds of things. When we weren't screwing, we talked about work.

But the worst part was knowing what would happen if Rory ever found out. I reasoned with myself that I would end the affair before it got too serious and way before Rory or her mom found out. When in reality I knew that I was already in way over my head. I had loved James from afar for two years. Now that I had him, I knew I wouldn't be able to give him up. And in a sick way, this also made me feel closer to Rory.

She's loved you since she was eleven years old. And I know that if you two ever got together, it would be a dream come true for her. That was the way it was for me, only I was acting out a disgusting schoolgirl fantasy. I was on the verge of destroying a family. And not just anyone's family, my best friend's family.

I hated myself throughout the whole thing, but I couldn't stop. Then Rory and I went off to UO and I tried to pretend to be happy. I even tried going out on a few dates, but I hated all those guys almost as much as I hated myself. Still, I kept pretending.

Then Rory asked me if I wanted to spend Thanksgiving with her family. I knew I could split my day between our house and Rory's house if I played my cards right with Mom. So I began to get excited at the prospect of possibly being alone with James again. But when Rory and I arrived the Saturday before Thanksgiving, he was very cold with me.

I thought he was just doing it so as not to arouse suspicion, but when I managed to catch him alone in the garage later that night, he told me very clearly that it was over between us. I insisted that it didn't have to be. That I could keep it a secret as long as he wanted me to, but he was adamant that the affair couldn't continue.

Still, I didn't believe him. I went inside the house and cried in the bathroom for a little while. Then I decided I'd just try to show him what he would be missing. I did pathetic things like sitting across from him at the dinner table and squeezing my breasts together just enough for them to appear larger. I would wait in the bathroom until I heard him coming out of his bedroom, then I'd walk out of the bathroom in nothing but a towel. I'm not certain, but I think Rory's mom began to notice what I was doing, and if that wasn't embarrassing enough, I began texting nude pictures of myself to the pay-as-you-go cell phone he bought over the summer. I think the number was disconnected, but I kept sending them in the hope that it wasn't.

When Thanksgiving finally came, I tried to sit next to him, but he decided to change seats so he could "carve the turkey at the head of the table." That was when it finally started to sink in that I had been used.

He never told me he loved me, but he always made it a point to tell me how beautiful I looked and how much he missed me when we were apart. I mistook this for love. But I was finally starting to realize that I had spent more than two years of my life loving someone who would never love me back. Even worse, I'd spent two years of my life dreaming of a life that would ruin my best friend if it were to come to fruition.

I've spent the past week absolutely sick with myself. I hate knowing that I grew up to be as sick as Dad. Absolutely no respect for the sanctity of marriage. I don't want to live with what I've done. And I don't want Rory to live with it either. That's why you can never show her this letter. And you need to promise me that you won't punish her for what James and I did.

I knew what I was doing, which only makes me even more

guilty. Please don't take it out on Rory. She's the victim in this whole fucked-up scenario. All she's ever done is love me and trust me, and I couldn't bear losing her over something like this.

I'm sorry that you had to find out this way. And I'm sorry that you're the one who had to find me. Please know that I didn't want to hurt you. I just didn't want to hurt Rory any more than I already have. Please help Mom and Rory get through this.

I love you always.

Hallie

Rory

Eight years ago, September 23rd

I HAVEN'T BEEN to the Gallery Theater since I was eight, so it's been eight years since the last time I came with my parents. Hallie has never been there in the five years since she moved to McMinnville with her mom and Houston, so I'm sure this visit will be more interesting than my last. Hallie and I get tickets for *Oklahoma* at 7:30 p.m., then we get in line behind a family of four to get inside the theater.

Hallie's quiet as she stares at the family, then she turns to me and leans in conspiratorially. "What is it like to love someone for as long as you've loved Houston?"

I'm a bit taken aback by this question. It's not the type of light banter that usually happens while standing in line at the theater. We reach the door and an usher takes our tickets, then leads us through the lobby and to our seats. The whole time, I sense Hallie anxiously awaiting my reply to her question. I don't know what's prompted her to ask me this, unless she has a crush that she hasn't told me about. But Hallie and I share everything.

The usher leads us to a pair of seats three rows back from the main stage. Once he's gone, Hallie turns to me with a smile on her face, awaiting my reply.

I shrug. "I don't know. I guess it's... crippling."

Her smile disappears. "Really?"

I think about Houston and how much I've missed him since he left for college last year. And how every time I see him at Hallie's house during holidays, my stomach cramps up and my thoughts get all jumbled. How I fall asleep most nights with thoughts of what it would be like to have those feelings reciprocated. And wake up with my heart broken when I realize the happiness I felt moments ago was just a dream.

"Really. It's awful."

Her shoulders slump as she lets out a soft sigh. "I want to be in love."

"With someone in particular?"

"No, I just want to feel like there's more than this, you know?"

I chuckle, feeling slightly confused. "No, I don't. More than what?"

She raises her hands, palms up, to indicate the stage cloaked in a velvety red curtain in front of us. "This! This place where we have to pretend to be someone we're not." She turns to me with a glint of electricity in her blue eyes. "It's not fair that you have to pretend you don't love my brother because he's nineteen and you're sixteen."

"Well, that's not the only reason. I asked you to never tell him because I don't want to get hurt. Then things would get awkward between you and me. Losing my best friend would be worse than never having Houston at all."

She stares at me for a moment, then her mouth curls into that signature half smile she shares with Houston. "That's completely corny."

I roll my eyes and stare at the stage. "Whatever. I guess I'm corny, but I stand by what I said. Your friendship is more important to me than taking a chance with Houston."

Her smile disappears and she sits back in her seat. "Friendship is more important." She repeats these words and I get a weird feeling she's not telling me something. "It's the *most* important thing."

"Without friendship, there's no love," I reply, though the phrase surprises even me.

Hallie nods in agreement. "No friendship, no love." She sighs as she ponders this, then she turns to me. "I think you and Houston are gonna end up together."

I try not to let her see how hearing these words come from her mouth makes me absurdly happy. "I doubt it. I'll never have the courage to make that happen."

"Maybe you won't, but maybe someone else will."

My eyes widen. "You wouldn't!"

"No, not me. But you never know. Maybe one of these days Houston will finally get a clue and make it happen on his own."

I let out an exasperated sigh. "It would be kind of hard for him to get a clue when he's ninety miles away."

"Yeah, but you'll be going to UO in a couple of years. Maybe you can show up at a party he's at and pretend to be drunk. Then he'll carry you back to your dorm and—*Ew*. I don't want to imagine that."

I give her a playful shove. "Stop it."

She laughs. "Yeah, you might not love him so much if you knew he used to sleep with my mom every time he got sick."

"That's adorable," I say, feigning a dreamy smile.

She cocks one eyebrow. "The last time he did it he was thirteen."

I imagine six-foot-four Houston lying in bed next to his petite momma. "Still adorable."

"You're sick."

I laugh and we continue chatting until the seats fill up around us. When the curtains part, I hold my breath, as if I'm one of the actors on the stage waiting for my cue. Well, according to Hallie, I *am* an actor. I guess she's right. I've gotten very good at pretending.

I pretend I don't love Houston. I pretend I'm going to UO so I can study, when the only reason I'm going is to be near him. And worst of all, I pretend not to be afraid that I'll never love anyone else.

After the show, Hallie and I walk home together arm-in-arm. It's a bit chilly, but the sky is clear, so we don't bother rushing home. We take our time, just breathing in the crisp autumn air and chatting about the play. We're a block away from my house when I remember that Hallie never answered my question earlier.

"Hey, you never told me if you have a crush on someone. Is that why you were asking me about Houston?"

A small part of me is hoping she asked me about him because he mentioned me to her. But I know that's next to impossible, so I make sure not to look too eager for her response. Still, the demure smile she's wearing as she thinks about this question is making me nervous. I wish she would just hurry up and answer me.

"No. I don't have a crush on anyone other than Justin Timberlake."

"Justin Timberlake doesn't count," I reply, shaking my head both at Hallie and at myself for thinking that Hallie would keep the identity of her crush from me. "He's an alien. It's not possible for a human to be born *that* hot, with *that* much talent."

We arrive in front of my two-story house on Evans Street and Hallie tucks her light-brown hair behind her ear as she stares at the upstairs windows. "Then I guess the answer is no. But that might change. We *are* juniors now."

"Is that supposed to be some sort of achievement? I thought turning sixteen was only a big deal in Texas."

"Everything's a big deal in Texas. Especially Justin Timberlake." She winks as she begins to walk away. "Call me later."

She heads off in the direction of her house around the corner and I can't help but wonder if Hallie is lying to me. She's stretched the truth before, but only to spare my feelings. Maybe Houston *did* say something about me, something about how I'll never have a chance with him.

My chest hurts just considering this. I stroll up the walkway toward the front steps and my dad opens the front door before I even reach the porch. "Hey, sweetheart. How was the show?"

I think about the amazing costumes and the energy of being that close to the performers. "It was great," I reply, taking off my jacket as I adjust to the warmth of the living room.

My dad takes my coat and I sit on the sofa to reflect on how much I liked the play. Then I think of the conversation Hallie and I had before the show about the importance of friendship. And I find solace in knowing that it doesn't matter if Houston asked Hallie about me, because what I said to her today is all that matters. I'd rather keep pretending not to love Houston than risk getting my heart broken and possibly losing her as a friend.

Because Hallie and I are more than friends. She's the sister I never had and the only person I don't have to pretend with.

No friendship, no love.

Houston

RORY CLOSES HER eyes when she finishes reading the letter. I hold my breath waiting for her response. The tears fall silently down her cheeks and I want to pull her in my arms and hold her until I've soaked up all her pain.

She opens her eyes and throws the letter at me as she leaps from the sofa and runs to the bathroom. Skippy and I race after her, but she slams the door to keep us out. The sound of her vomiting makes my stomach ache. But the sobs that come between each chorus of retching make me absolutely sick with myself.

I knock on the door when I hear a few seconds of silence, but her response echoes in the toilet bowl. "Go away!"

She's dry heaving now, but she manages to tell me to get out a couple more times. If it were anyone but Rory I would listen. I push the bathroom door open slowly and she's sobbing with her cheek resting on her arm, which is resting on the toilet seat. Skippy peeks inside the bathroom, sees her near the toilet, then turns around to go back to the living room.

I kneel next to her and she looks up at me, her eyes full of absolute despair. "I'm sorry I didn't show you the letter sooner," I begin, "but you can't tell me you don't understand why."

She covers her mouth as she sits up and leans back against the tub. "I don't understand any of this." Her shoulders fold inward as she tries to hold back the sobbing and retching. "And I don't know if I even *want* to understand it. I'm so disgusted with myself. I'm so stupid."

"You're not stupid. You're the only smart person in this whole fucked-up situation."

"No, I'm an idiot. I've spent thirteen years loving someone who was incapable of loving me. How, Houston? How could you pretend to love me for so long?"

I clench my jaw as I look into her eyes. "I wasn't pretending," I reply. "I couldn't ask you to choose between me and your father. Just because our relationship was built on a lie, it doesn't mean I didn't love the fuck out of you... I still do and I always will."

She rests her elbows on her knees and closes her eyes as she covers her face. "I knew you were hiding something from me, but I never expected this." She draws in a long, stuttered breath, then she looks up at me with a question in her eyes. "You said our relationship was built on a lie. What does that mean?"

I let out a deep sigh as I prepare to tell her the most damaging secret of them all. "When I asked you to move in with me, I hadn't read Hallie's letter yet. But after we went back to my apartment, I sat in the bathroom with the letter and tried not to punch the mirror as I read Hallie's words. I've never been so mad in my life. I wanted to burst into the bedroom where you were sleeping and take my anger out on you even though Hallie had just begged me not to in that letter."

Rory shakes her head as she covers her face again. I wish her father were here to see what a frightening mess all of us have made of this beautiful girl. This innocent girl whose only sin was to love and trust with all her heart.

"But I decided that instead of hurting you right there and then, I would bide my time. And I'd hurt you when you least expected it. I wanted you to hurt as much as Hallie did, then maybe your dad would feel the gravity of what he'd done to my sister. Maybe then he'd feel just a *drop* of the pain I was feeling."

She looks up at me, her eyes wide with shock. "That's why you broke up with me when I told you about the pregnancy? To *destroy* me?"

I shake my head adamantly. "No, you don't understand. Initially, I wanted to hurt you. But it only took a couple of days for the anger to subside. And in less than a month, I had fallen so utterly and completely in love with you, Rory.

"When you told me about the baby, I broke up with you because I was afraid if we got married, and I had to see your father walking you down the aisle or holding our child, I wouldn't be able to keep on lying to you. But I knew the truth would knock the stilts out from underneath us and we'd fall so hard we might never get up. I didn't want to ruin you. All I ever wanted was for you to move on."

"Move on?" Her hands tremble as she wipes the tears from her chin. "How was I supposed to do that when you were holding on to the one thing that would give me closure?"

"I'm so sorry I didn't show you the letter. It's the biggest regret of my life."

"Your biggest regret?" She shakes her head as if she can't believe what's she's hearing. "Fuck you and your regrets. Your regrets ruined me. Get out."

I reach for her face and she smacks my hand away. "I know you hate me right now, but this isn't over."

"Yes, it is." She rises from the floor and I follow her out of the bathroom. "This is where it ends." She stops just inside the front door, her lips trembling as she presses them together and looks me in the eye. "Good-bye, Houston."

"We'll always make it back to each other."

"Back to *what*? There's nothing left."

Stepping forward, I take her face in my hands. "Back to *us*. This isn't the end of us, Rory. You know it as well as I do." My lips brush softly over the tracks of tears glistening on her supple skin and she lets out a muffled sob. "The world can fall to pieces around us, but in the end, we'll always make it back to us."

She grabs my wrists as I kiss the corner of her mouth. "No, Houston, don't."

"We're the only thing that makes sense in all of this." I kiss her again and she whimpers. "Just give me some time to make this right."

Tangling my fingers in her silky hair, I kiss her tenderly. Her lips are salty and moist with tears, but she kisses me back. I want to lift her up and carry her to the bedroom, but I don't want to make this even more difficult. After today, Rory and I will have to go back to being strangers until I can figure a safe way out of my marriage.

She groans as she pushes me away and whispers, "Stop." Her gaze is fixed on Hallie's letter and the Sierra Nevada box where I left them on the coffee table. "Get out, Houston. And don't ever knock on my door again. Ever."

I stare at the box on the table and consider taking it

with me—she did try to give it back to me earlier—but I decide to leave it. Telling Rory the truth doesn't change the fact that the ring is hers. If she doesn't want it, neither do I.

I also want to grab the letter. It's been such an important part of my life for the past five and a half years. It's my last connection to my baby sister. It's proof of her suffering. But I think that's exactly why I have to leave it with Rory.

I may have loved Hallie, but Rory knew and loved her like no one else. Rory deserves to hold on to that letter so she can seek the answers she needs to finally find some peace. I only hope I'll be there when that happens.

I sigh as I reach for the doorknob. "You'll always be the deepest scar on my heart."

Rory

Seven weeks later

THE LINE FOR the wine tasting is so long it extends from the bar, out along the glass walls enclosing this area from the rest of the market, and snakes around the glass until it reaches the sidewalk outside. The grand opening of Zucker's Café & Wine Bar looks like it's going to be a huge success. After the stress of the past seven weeks, I should be excited for all the preparation to finally be over. But I can't think of anything else right now except the guy staring at me from where he stands at the front of the line of customers.

He looks a little nervous, with his hands tucked in his pockets and a bashful smile lighting up his boyish good looks. I smile at him as Bella and I walk in and take our place behind the bar. He beams and I shake my head as I wonder how someone can be born with such a perfect smile.

"I'll take the first person in line," I say, looking straight at him. He steps forward as Bella takes the customer behind him. "What can I help you with, sir?"

He scratches his beard as he reads the options on the menu board on the wall behind me. "I'll take a bottle of Lagunitas IPA and"—he cocks an eyebrow and I wait for him to finish—"a date to my brother's annual Hipster Halloween party next Saturday."

I raise my eyebrows. "That's a tall order. Let me get your beer first." I grab his beer out of the cooler behind me, then I pop the top off and set it down in front of him on top of a cocktail napkin. "That will be $7.50."

He hands me a ten-dollar bill and tells me to keep the change. "And the party?"

"Who's going to be there?"

"Just a bunch of people wearing irony as if it didn't go out of style last year."

"Irony is so over!"

He laughs at my reference to *Portlandia*. "Looks like you'll fit right in."

I sigh as I look at the impatient line of thirsty patrons waiting behind him. "Okay, but you have to promise not to leave my side. I'm terrible at parties. I'm… way out of practice."

"Don't worry. I'll stick to you like a beard on a

hipster."

He winks at me as he sets off to sit at a small table in the corner. I steal glances at him every few customers and every once in a while I catch him looking in my direction. His presence is making me a little nervous. I keep wondering if either Houston or Troy are going to show up for the grand opening.

I haven't seen Houston since he brought Hallie's letter to me seven weeks ago. Troy has been handling the setup of the beer taps. I don't know if this is because Houston is trying to respect my desire to not see him or because he's the one who doesn't want to see me. But seeing Troy six times in the past seven weeks has been more than enough reminders.

Every time Troy walked into the bar, I practically held my breath the entire time he was here. I was just waiting for him to say something about Houston. Sometimes, I'd try to guess what he might say, but that became too painful a game to play. What if Troy broke his silence only to tell me that Houston and his wife were now living happily ever after?

Just imagining this scenario makes me sick with emotional agony. And the nausea only worsens when I realize how deeply I'm still in love with Houston. And how, no matter how toxic things got between us, the good still outweighs the bad in my lovesick recollection.

After three hours and forty minutes without a break in the line of customers, Bella and I are relieved by Benji and Hernando, the only person at the grand opening with actual bartending experience. Bella makes herself a skinny latte and I grab an iced green tea before heading over to join Liam at his table.

"Those are some impressive beer pouring skills," he remarks.

"It's all in the wrist." I sigh as my aching feet tingle with relief when I sit down. "I'm sorry I haven't been answering your calls."

"Or texts, but who's keeping track?" He smiles as he stares at the empty beer bottle on the table. "I figured you had a lot on your mind, and you did respond that one time to tell me you were okay, so I probably should have taken the hint. I guess I'm just a glutton for punishment."

"It's been a weird seven weeks."

"Want to talk about it?"

I look up from my iced tea, and the inquisitive expression on his face makes me want to tell him everything, but I don't want to scare him away. Plus, my coffee break is nowhere near long enough to explain how I fell in love with a boy thirteen years ago and he, along with my best friend, proceeded to smash my heart into a billion pieces. Or how I looked up to my father as a role model most of my life and how, until seven weeks ago, I was unable to comprehend why he's hardly spoken to me in the past five years. Or how my mother could possibly think I didn't want to know her suspicions about Hallie. Basically, I don't have enough time to tell Liam how everyone I've ever given my heart to managed to stomp all over it.

"I think that conversation should be saved for a moment when you have about ninety-two hours to spare."

He chuckles. "I'll have to check my calendar, but I think I can fit you in next month."

"Lucky you." I take another sip from my tea, then I sit back in my wooden chair. "Why do you like me?"

He laughs and I realize how weird that must sound to him.

"I'm serious," I insist. "I'm a hot mess."

"That's probably why I like you," he replies. "I like my girls like I like my… girls: hot and messy."

"That's an amazing analogy."

"What can I say? When I was in college, I was partnered up with this really smart girl who taught me how to construct the perfect sentence."

"Really? So what's the perfect sentence?"

He smiles and leans forward as if he's about to divulge a secret. "Then, she let it go."

I don't know if it was his intention, but these five simple words stir a newfound energy inside me. A sudden awareness that I don't have to tell Liam anything about Houston. Liam can be my fresh start. All I have to do is let it go.

I smile as I rise from the table. "Sounds like a

triumphant last line in a book."

"Feel free to use it."

I nod as I turn to leave. "I just might."

As I walk back to the bar, I glance at Liam over my shoulder, but he's already out of his chair and heading toward the recycling bins near the coffee prep station. I turn back toward the bar, but something I see out of the corner of my eye makes my heart stop. I whip my head around to get a better look, but no one's there.

I shake my head in disbelief. A half a second ago Houston was standing right there near the entrance. I can still see the green Barley Legal hoodie and the soft light bouncing off his golden-brown hair. But now he's gone.

Am I going crazy?

I rush back to the bar before anyone realizes how disturbed I am. Liam leaves the store and I spend the rest of the night trying not to sweat as I slide glass after glass of beer and wine across the bar. Bella and Benji offer to give me a ride when we leave the store at eleven p.m., but I decline their offer and set off on my own.

I don't mind walking the streets of Goose Hollow late at night. Besides, it gives me a chance to walk off some of the leftover anxiety from seeing Houston's ghost.

I stroll casually through the misty rain, inhaling deep breaths of cleansing Oregon air as I contemplate how much of the truth I should share with Liam and where this new adventure may take me. Maybe Liam will be the equivalent of Houston's PTSD therapy. Perhaps he'll help me forget everything I've lost and found.

I was eighteen when I got lost in Houston, and in him I found myself. They say love is just two souls recognizing each other. With Houston and me it was more like two souls staring into a mirror, my left hand aligned with his right, our hearts skipping a beat at the same moment, our lungs choking on the same noxious air, our scars as perfectly aligned as mountains and fault lines. If ever two souls were perfectly right and perfectly wrong for each other, it would be us.

Us.

I guess the story of *us* ends here.

But Hallie's story continues. And I won't rest until I know her truth inside and out.

Right now, all I know is that Hallie was drowning, but she was too afraid to reach for a lifeline. As heartbroken as I am that she didn't give me the opportunity to understand her, I'm even more grateful to her for loving me enough to try to protect me in her last moments. And for teaching me the most important lesson I've ever learned.

You can't erase love without erasing yourself.

Acknowledgments

This book was a collaborative labor of love. And I have never had so many people to thank, so please bear with me.

My beta readers: Sarah Arndt, Kristin Shaw, Paula Jackman, Cathy Archer, and Carrie Raasch. You all went above and beyond on this book, especially my "brainstormers" who braved the spoilers so they could better understand the characters and the story arc. I loved working on *The Way We Fall* with you, even when we disagreed and argued over the characters actions and motivations. Having people in my corner who know the story and characters like I do is an invaluable resource and I am eternally grateful that I get to write books with such an awesome group of women.

Sarah Hansen. Thank you for squeezing me in and making last minute changes to this book cover instead of telling me to suck it. This design was totally your vision, and I couldn't be happier. The image of Houston's hand reaching for the female hand, which symbolizes the three women in his life he couldn't save, gives me chills.

Big thanks to my editor, Jessica Anderson of Red Adept Edits. Thank you for your attention to detail and for getting this project done in record time. Can't wait to work on the next one!

More huge thanks to my proofreader, Marianne Tatom. I am never more happy to discover how terrible my grammar and proofreading skills are as when I get my marked-up manuscript back from you. You are remarkable at what you do.

Thank you to Tamara Paulin and Deanna Roy for being the backbone of my author support system. The daily interaction and word c(o)unt races keep me *somewhat* sane.

Thank you to all the bloggers who shared *The Way We Fall* cover reveal and preorder links and those who participated in the blog tour and release activities. And a big thank you to Nazarea Andrews and Inkslinger PR for handling this launch.

To the readers who have encouraged me and shared their excitement for the release of *The Way We Fall,* and *all* my books, you are the ones that keep me going on the days when I doubt myself. If you stick with me, I'll stick with you.

A huge thank-you to the state of Oregon, particularly the city of Portland. Being one of the three states I've lived in, Oregon has been on my list of book settings to tackle for a long time. I am so happy I finally got to revisit Oregon. And I'm very proud to bring some attention to the magical hipster-land that is Beertown. I apologize if I changed the facts a bit (*ahem*, pet policy at Portland Towers) to suit my fictional world.

To Arielle, who not only helped me develop the idea for this novel, you also encouraged me to follow my inspiration at a time when I wanted very much to give up on writing epic love stories. There is really no one who encourages me more than you do. I love you and I'm proud of you, always.

Also by Cassia Leo

CONTEMPORARY ROMANCE

Forever Ours (Shattered Hearts #1)

Relentless (Shattered Hearts #2)

Pieces of You (Shattered Hearts #3)

Bring Me Home (Shattered Hearts #4)

Abandon (Shattered Hearts #5)

Chasing Abby (Shattered Hearts #6)

Black Box (stand-alone novel)

EROTIC ROMANCE

KNOX Series

LUKE Series

CHASE Series

UNMASKED Series

Edible: The Sex Tape (A Short Story)

PARANORMAL ROMANCE

Parallel Spirits (Carrier Spirits #1)

About the Author

New York Times and *USA Today* bestselling author Cassia Leo loves her coffee, chocolate, and margaritas with salt. When she's not writing, she spends way too much time watching old reruns of *Friends* and *Sex and the City*. When she's not watching reruns, she's usually enjoying the California sunshine or reading – sometimes both.

31100861R10190

Made in the USA
San Bernardino, CA
02 March 2016